The Truth Sayer

CR
F
PRU

Other books by Sally Prue

Cold Tom
The Devil's Toenail
Ryland's Footsteps
Goldkeeper

The Truth Sayer

SALLY PRUE

OXFORD
UNIVERSITY PRESS

OXFORD
UNIVERSITY PRESS

Great Clarendon Street, Oxford OX2 6DP

Oxford University Press is a department of the University of Oxford.
It furthers the University's objective of excellence in research, scholarship,
and education by publishing worldwide in

Oxford New York

Auckland Cape Town Dar es Salaam Hong Kong Karachi
Kuala Lumpur Madrid Melbourne Mexico City Nairobi
New Delhi Shanghai Taipei Toronto

With offices in

Argentina Austria Brazil Chile Czech Republic France Greece
Guatemala Hungary Italy Japan Poland Portugal Singapore
South Korea Switzerland Thailand Turkey Ukraine Vietnam

Oxford is a registered trade mark of Oxford University Press
in the UK and in certain other countries

British Library Cataloguing in Publication Data
Data available

ISBN 978-0-19-275440-0

3 5 7 9 10 8 6 4 2

Typeset in Sabon by TnQ Books and Journals Pvt. Ltd.,
Chennai, India

Printed in Great Britain
by Cox & Wyman Ltd, Reading, Berkshire

Nian

1

They came for Nian on the day of the hay feast.

He saw the men as they toiled up to the farm, but he was working in the high fields and he thought nothing of it.

Nian's feast clothes were laid out on his sleeping mat. He shrugged himself into his tunic and tied his sash carefully. It was edged in scarlet to show he was the eldest son, and he was proud of it.

His mother caught him as he was slipping down the stairs and inflicted a severe hair-combing on him.

'We've visitors,' Mother told him, between his yelps of anguish. 'So you've got to look respectable.'

'But they're only our own people,' objected Nian, wincing against the tug of the comb. 'They won't recognize me if I look respectable.'

Mother gave Nian's hair one last tug and then stood back to view him; and her face was shadowed with something more serious than the worry of preparing the feast.

'It's not just our people,' she said. 'I only wish it were. Nian, some Tarhun have come.'

And at that all the joy of the harvest and the feast shrivelled away inside him.

Tarhun had come.

'Have they come looking for boys?' he asked.

Mother nodded slowly.

'Nian,' she said, 'Nian, you won't—'

'What?' he asked fiercely.

But Mother only shook her head.

'Go to your grandmother,' she said. 'She needs help with setting out the feast. And be careful of your clothes, Nian, they took me an age to iron. Be *careful*.'

But Nian didn't go down to the kitchen: instead he slipped out and across the yard to the suntrap warmth of the privy. He needed to think.

Tarhun had come. That was a disaster—or would be, unless he was very careful: because they had come for him.

That was the Tarhun's job: they came searching for boys who had second sight, or could read minds. Nian had known this since he was quite small. One day his grandmother had overheard him telling his sister Miri when the rain would stop. Grandy had swooped on him and carried him, kicking, to her small room. Then she'd stood him in front of her and told him what happened to little boys who told the future. They were taken away to the top of the Holy Mountain, which was even higher and colder than the shining green mountains that surrounded the valley, and they were never seen again.

Grandy was fierce that day, like a cloud-lynx; and she'd sent him to his sleeping mat without his supper so he'd remember what she'd said.

Nian was careful not to tell the future after that. Glimpses of it would come sometimes, fleetingly, as he was waking up, but mostly he kept a sort of screen down inside his head so that visions of the future didn't come into the everyday part of his mind. No one ever spoke of his gift, and Nian might have thought that Grandy had kept it a secret—except that sometimes, perhaps when someone was going on a journey, his father would wonder aloud what the weather was going to be. And then Nian would look into the future to check for the violent storms that sometimes rolled in from the south.

Lords' Storms, they were called: for the men on the Holy Mountain, the Lords of Truth, had the power to deflect any bad weather that threatened them.

Father would pretend that what Nian saw was a guess.

But there was no need to worry about the Tarhun. No one here would betray him. And the Tarhun had no powers to find him out, for the men with powers, the Lords, never left the Holy Mountain. There was nothing to be afraid of, as long as he was careful.

And his mother had told him to be careful.

Grandy was bringing out the new puffed ovals of bread from the oven when Nian entered the kitchen. Grandy's face was pink with heat from the fire, but her eyes were cold with fear.

3

'And where have you been?' she demanded, sounding somehow not quite like herself. 'Skulking out in the yard instead of lending a hand. You ought to be ashamed of yourself!'

She was angry because she was afraid, but still it wasn't fair to take it out on Nian.

'I *have* come to lend a hand,' he said stiffly.

But Grandy only snorted.

'Yes—when you are too late to be of any use!' she snapped. 'Here,' she went on, pushing the hot loaves onto a platter with quick flicks of her fingers. 'Take this into the Hall. And you may as well stay there, for you're too late to do any good here!'

Nian took the platter resentfully and shouldered his way through the swing door. The farm people were milling about in the yard waiting for the welcoming bell. In the Hall, everything was nearly ready. Mother was fussing about with one of the jugs of flowers, and Miri was going round straightening plates with one hand and re-pinning her headcloth with the other.

And sitting in the corner were three strangers.

Nian's heart thumped warningly. The strangers wore tunics of red skin, and they had cunning little eyes that seemed already to know his secrets. *Tarhun.*

Mother seized the platter of bread and put it exactly in the middle of the High Table.

'Nian,' said Father, from the other end of the Hall. 'You are to sit at my right hand today, beside our guests the Tarhun. It is time you learned to entertain visitors.'

4

I hate the Tarhun, thought Nian, though he felt a spark of pride.

'And now we must ring the welcoming bell,' went on Father. 'And that,' he said, smiling at Tan, 'is the job of the *youngest* child.'

'Just *seven* times, Tan,' Mother reminded him, hastily, as Tan, who had been waiting for this moment all day, raised the mallet to give the bell the biggest bashing it had ever had.

Miri put her hands to her ears, Mother set her teeth, and Father raised his own hands in the sign of greeting that a host makes when his doors are opened at a feast.

Tang! Tang! Tang! Tang! Tang! Tang! Tang!

The sound made Nian's ears buzz. The doors were being pushed open by the cheerful jostling crowd of farm-people, but Nian found himself remembering those other bells, the death-bells, that had rung over his uncle's grave.

But no one else was remembering them.

'Welcome, my friends,' said Father, to his people. 'For now is the season to be merry.'

And the Tarhun rose as one and advanced upon the food-laden table.

11

The Tarhun ate like men who had been hunting. They ate so solidly that there was no point in talking to them. All Nian had to do was pass them dish after dish and pretend not to be disgusted at their table manners. When he looked into the Tarhun's little eyes, that lay embedded within rolls of greasy fat, he understood why his father had placed him next to them. These were sly, suspicious men. They might be too busy snuffling after secrets hidden in corners to see what was under their noses.

The Tarhun hung their faces over their plates and ate and ate, but in the end even the fattest of them had to lean back to allow his belches to rise. It was then that Nian realized he could sense his parents' fear. It was fizzing into the air around him and making his nose itch.

That was so interesting that the attack of the Tarhun took him by surprise.

'So, Master,' said the very fattest of them, 'which of your sons has the gifts?'

Nian wanted very much to tell the Tarhun that his brother Tan wasn't gifted at anything. But he kept his mouth shut.

Father cut a hay-apple neatly into halves.

'Neither, that I know of,' he said calmly. 'Not gifted in Wisdom, anyway. Nian here is a fine active boy, though. He's been helping cut the hay.'

That annoyed the Tarhun—and it was a good thing to annoy them, because anger would cloud their minds.

'We aren't looking for farmhands!' the fattest one snapped. 'We're looking for Lords of Truth!'

'The world is desperately in need of boys to enter the holy House,' put in the tallest of the Tarhun, who had a nasty little moustache. 'The Lords of Truth are dying one by one. Who will keep the world safe from invasion if there are no boys to follow them? Who will keep the Lords' Wisdom alive until the Truth Sayer comes?'

Father nodded sympathetically.

'Who indeed,' he said. 'But I'm afraid we can't help you here. Have you tried—'

'Do you take us for fools?' demanded the fattest of the Tarhun, scowling. 'Do you think we don't know that every year for the last five years you have had the best harvests in the whole valley? That you gathered your frostberries the day before the snows came, even though you had to ripen most of them indoors? How can you account for that, except by the fact that one of your children has second sight?'

A chill ran through Nian. Someone had given the Tarhun information, then, but not on purpose, probably, for the people of the valleys were simple, trusting folk, and the Tarhun were cunning.

7

Father shrugged.

'Some might call it skill,' he remarked, mildly, but Nian felt the cold spurt of fear that fizzed from him. It was so strong it made Nian sneeze.

'Aye, and whose skill?' demanded the third Tarhun, who was bald apart from his ponytail. 'That's what we need to know!'

He looked down the table and beckoned impatiently to Tan, who was a big shambling boy for his age, and had sometimes even been mistaken for the elder son. 'Here!' he barked. 'Come here, boy!'

Tan gave a glance at his father, then he rose, reluctantly, and made his slow way to where the Tarhun sat.

'Tell me,' the man said. 'What do I hold in my hand?'

Tan gazed doubtfully at the outstretched fist; then he shook his head.

'I don't know, sir,' he said.

But then the Tarhun put his other hand in his pocket and drew out a marble of coloured glass. It was a very beautiful marble, with swirls of red inside the sphere. Nian felt a small longing for it himself; in Tan, who was a whole year younger than him, Nian saw that the longing to possess it was painful and severe.

'If you could tell me,' said the Tarhun, coaxingly, 'I would give you this to keep.' And he touched the marble so that it shone for a moment with deep wine-coloured fire.

Tan's eyes were wide and wistful.

8

'A grindlenut,' he said, guessing.

The Tarhun started violently, then he turned to his companions and they all threw up their hands in something like wonder—except for the hand which had been held out to Tan, which was plunged back into the owner's pocket.

'What marvellous gifts the boy has!' exclaimed the tallest one, his voice high with false surprise. 'Take the marble, my dear boy! You have won it fairly.'

Tan's hand closed swiftly over the glowing sphere.

Nian looked doubtfully at his father, for this was all a cheat. Tan *wasn't* gifted: Tan wasn't gifted at anything.

Father gave a small smile.

'That was just a lucky guess,' he said, polite, but firm. 'That's no proof of anything.'

The fattest of the Tarhun shook his head.

'You are much too modest,' he replied. '*Much* too modest. Why, the boy has passed the test quite *brilliantly*! We will take him with us tomorrow, and he will enter the House of Truth. What an honour for your house!'

Everyone gasped, except Nian. Nian couldn't even breathe, because all his insides had fallen away into nothingness. He understood the cheat, now. He looked up at the high beams of his father's hall, and he knew that he would have to leave: leave everything and everyone he had ever cared about. How could he do that?

Tan was cowering like a grain-pig. He was young for his age, the baby of the family, and he was on the point of howling. Nian couldn't let them take Tan.

9

But that meant he had no choice. No choice at all.

There were weights on his lips, but he had to speak even though it would mean he'd be banished from everything he loved for ever.

'Tan doesn't have any gifts,' he said, his voice shrill with misery and anger. 'I am the gifted one. I can tell the future, and I can read minds a little: there was nothing in the hand you held out to Tan.'

The men of the Tarhun exchanged oily, smug, triumphant glances. And then they all rose to their feet and they bowed to Nian, hands to their hollow hearts.

'Then, Lord,' said the fattest one, greasily, 'we shall take you, instead.'

Jacob

1

Jacob Rush had never been one for worrying. After all, what did it *matter* if the front room was full of frenzied tribal drumming? True, it could be a bit of a pain if you were trying to watch telly, but turning up the volume pretty much sorted that out. And as for the shrieking . . . well, it could be a bit of a shock if you weren't expecting it, but you had to remember that those weren't *necessarily* screams of agony. People screamed for all sorts of reasons, like when the hot water ran out in the shower.

An extra shrill screech skewered its way through the wall to the back room, where the family were eating. Dad twitched so horribly he spilled his tea.

'Now look what you've done,' said Nan, tetchily, through a mouthful of Eccles cake, 'all over my best cloth.'

Mum jumped up.

'I'll soon mop that up,' she said. 'I was going to wash the cloth tomorrow, anyway. So no harm done.'

Exactly. No harm done. No point in worrying. After all, you only had to look at Dad to see where worrying got you. Mind you, it was lucky that none of the others were able to hear all the stuff that was coming out of the front room, or there really would have been trouble.

Jacob took a swig of his orange juice and wondered for the thousandth time why it was that only he and Dad could hear the front room noises that had been a part of practically every day of his life. It must be something genetic, he supposed, or else some sort of hereditary curse.

The drumming wasn't that loud, really, but it was making everything on the table tremble slowly across the cloth.

Nan shoved the salt cellar back in its place.

'Blessed lorries, coming over from the continent and making the whole blooming house shake!' she muttered.

Dad was gnawing his knuckles, now, and Jacob had to admit it *could* be a bit off-putting listening to tribal sacrifices during tea—though it wasn't as though the sacrifices were actually there. He'd quite often checked the front room when it sounded as if something interesting was going on in the *Wherevers*, as he thought of them, but there was never anything to see at all.

A long and very accomplished drum roll came through the wall, and then a moment of silence. Then, unmistakably, an axe fell. Even Jacob flinched a bit at that, and Dad let out a sort of gasping half-groan that earned him an eye-rolling from Jacob's big sister Robyn.

Dad had too much imagination, that was the trouble, and it didn't help that he was at home all day because he wasn't well. Jacob did at least get to go to school, where things were boring, but explainable (except algebra, which was just boring), but Dad was stuck here the whole time with the *Wherevers*, worrying that he was round the twist.

Jacob had tried to talk to Dad about the *Wherevers* once or twice, but Dad always panicked so badly at the mere mention of Other Worlds that Jacob had always had to let matters rest.

But things could be worse. Personally, Jacob didn't find these tribal ceremonies half as distracting as the sounds of some of the other *Wherevers* that came out of the front room chimney breast. He actually enjoyed the drumming, and even the screaming wasn't as bad as, for example, the howling wolves, the creaking of the ship in the mighty sea, or, especially, the beginner violin group. It really was a jolly good thing that none of the *Wherevers* stayed with them for more than a few days or so at a time.

You had to look on the bright side.

Mum and Nan and Robyn were munching away, oblivious.

Jacob shrugged, and helped himself to a bit of fruit loaf.

There was no point in worrying.

|||

The journey to the Holy Mountain took seven days, and Nian escaped seven times. He tried everything he knew. He tried hiding in a crack of green rock; climbing a crag during the night; throwing rocks to make it sound as if he'd jumped into the lake; actually jumping into the lake; starting an avalanche; putting poppy juice in the Tarhun's food; and even just plain, desperate running. But the Tarhun were well-versed in the tricks of boys taken against their will. Nian was caught every time, and each time the Tarhun mocked him for his failure.

Nian hated the Tarhun. He hated the Tarhun with a fervour that was white-hot. He nursed his hatred and exulted in it with all his strength, because it was the only thing that stopped him breaking down in tears of utter despair.

'My Lord,' said the fattest of the Tarhun, pointing, on the afternoon of the seventh day. 'There is the House of Truth.'

Nian looked on up the track. Not far away a high wall encircled the green rocky peak of the mountain. The House of Truth was bigger than anything Nian had ever seen or dreamed of, and in the light of the suns the walls gleamed like cliffs of ice. A voice said:

'It is the greatest building in the world, Lord.' But somewhere between the white walls and the tears of anger and self-pity that stung Nian's eyes he seemed to see the people of his home. To each of them, to Mother, to Father, to Grandy, to Miri, to Tan and to all the others he had said the same thing. He'd said *Do not forget me because I'll be back*. And to Tan he'd given his scarlet-piped sash, because now Tan had to be the eldest son.

'Look after it,' Nian had told him, very sternly. 'For when I come back I'll need it again.'

The door of the House of Truth was not large, but it was made of bronzewood and iron.

'Knock, Lord,' said the tallest of the Tarhun. 'All who wish to enter must beg admittance.'

Nian gave him a smouldering glare.

'Even you are not stupid enough to think I wish to enter,' he said.

The Tarhun tut-tutted mildly, and stepped forward to knock on the door with his staff.

'Come,' he said, reasonably. 'Being received into the House is a great honour, Lord.'

'And that is why you have to bring people here by force,' said Nian, scowling.

But the Tarhun only smiled their sly, smug smiles. Nian would have turned and run away again, except that it would be futile, and because of the humiliation of being caught.

Below him the valleys were lush and green in the light of the lowering suns; his home was out of sight, now, and the knowledge that he would probably never see it again made new tears rise in his eyes.

The door creaked open, and Nian knew that many important parts of himself were about to die.

But there was nothing he could do to stop it.

He took one last breath of the air of freedom, and one last lingering look at the valleys that had held his whole life—and then he stepped over the threshold, and the door thudded shut behind him.

It was dark in the House of Truth, and the air was sour with the smell of the Tarhun's red-dyed tunics.

But there was something else, as well. Yes. Something close by was giving out wave upon wave of . . . *something*. And it was something so hugely strong that it would have frightened the life out of Nian if he had not already been hating the Tarhun with all his strength.

'We must bid you farewell, here, Lord,' said the bald Tarhun, slimily. 'For you will make your home in the Inner House, where none of the Tarhun may enter.'

They all compressed their paunches in grotesque bows.

'Farewell, Lord,' they said, stretching the greasy corners of their mouths upwards.

Nian hated them.

16

'I don't want you to fare well,' he said, bitterly. 'It'd be better if you fell over a precipice tonight than that you trapped any more boys with your cheating.'

But they only laughed, smugly and triumphantly, and Nian's anger flared hotter than ever.

'This is the path to the Inner House,' said the tallest of the Tarhun, pushing open another door, and Nian screwed up his grey eyes at the sudden brightness. Across a stretch of bare green rock was a building that shone hard and white in the light of the Great Sun. This was where the power was coming from: a billow of it gusted at him, dry, and pulsing, like the beating of a dead heart. He hated it. He hated this mountain, and he hated the House; most of all he hated these men, the Tarhun and the Lords of Truth, who'd brought him here and destroyed his life.

'I'll escape,' he said, loudly and defiantly. 'I'll run away and go home. And if you bring me back I'll run away again. I'll escape!'

And then blindly, miserably, he stumbled forward through the doorway.

||||

The path was a hundred paces long, and with every step Nian said to himself, *I'll escape.* He went slowly, looking out for crumbled stonework, straggles of fire-ivy, a window, anything to help him in a climb. The Outer House, where the Tarhun lived, seemed to form a massive circle round the inner one like the curtain wall of a castle. There were no windows that Nian could see, but here and there the stonework was decayed enough to provide a toehold.

The Inner House in front of him seemed to be circular, too, for the long wall curved gently away on both sides. Nian prowled grimly along the path, and with every step the power from the House pushed at him. He would have turned aside and tried climbing out over the walls of the Outer House straight away—but it was too late. He was being watched.

There was a man standing in a doorway at the far end of the path. He was shrunken with age, and so thin that his face was hardly more than a skull.

Nian came to an uncertain halt.

'Welcome,' said the old man, but his face was empty.

I'll escape, thought Nian, fiercely.

'I am Tarq, the pupil-father,' went on the old man, as gentle as frost, 'and this is your home, for ever. Come into the House, my son.'

Nian unwillingly stepped over the threshold—and as he did, the power of the place fell on him. It closed round him smotheringly, softly, like an invisible fleece. Nian put up his hands to tear away a space so he could breathe, but his hands couldn't get a grip on it. He stepped backwards hastily, but it followed him, clung to him, settled softly and irresistibly against his skin.

And now he couldn't hold his breath any more: he gasped hugely and the power slipped down his throat with the air. It smelt like—he searched his mind—like the hot iron Mother used to smooth the clothes at home. Yes, that was right: the reason his heart was beating so fast was because he was reminded of the dangerous iron at home.

Tarq was watching him carefully.

'Does something trouble you, my son?' he asked.

Nian opened his mouth to say, *I hate every stone of this place*. But it was somehow hard to say that. It was suddenly hard to say anything.

Tarq's skull-face widened itself into a smile.

'This House is strange to you, my son, but it will not be strange for long. Come, we shall go to the schoolrooms.'

Nian had heard of schools. The valley's animal doctor had told him dreadful tales of cold classrooms and terrifying masters. Nian looked sideways at Tarq. The old man seemed as mild as milk—but even so, with every difficult breath that Nian took, the House's force was invading him. It was a quiet, stealthy thing, this force, but it filled Nian with terror, for it felt as if it was dissolving all his bones.

Tarq led Nian along a wide white corridor. The House was so still that it took a real effort to speak against the silence, and even more effort to think violent thoughts about escape.

'Is there no one else here?' Nian asked, for the place felt empty, except perhaps for the watching eyes of ghosts.

'There are others, my son, but they are turning aside a storm,' the old man replied. 'There is snow to the east, and it will take much of our Wisdom to divert it.'

It took a struggle not to be impressed, but then Nian remembered his uncle, frozen to death in the snow that had swept northwards last year on a mild and westerly wind.

A Lords' Storm.

His hatred flared again.

Tarq led him through the arch of a doorway into a wide room and Nian halted in surprise, for here there was no floor, but instead a deep pool. Columns rose through it to join each other in a myriad domes.

'You will bathe, now,' said Tarq.

Nian looked from the pool to the old man and back again. The water had the clearness of the iciest stream, and surely only a fool bathed on a mountain top.

But, somehow, he found himself taking off his clothes.

He stood, miserable and shivering, on the edge of the pool.

'I might freeze to death,' he said. He meant it to sound accusing, but somehow it came out merely pitiful.

'No, my son,' said Tarq, placidly, 'for I shall heat the water with the force of my Wisdom. You will learn how to do it for yourself, in time. But for today . . . '

Tarq stretched out his hands towards the water and let his pale eyes close. Nian was strongly tempted to give him a shove into the pool and make a run for it, but a moment later he was ducking hastily away from a stream of something that was rushing in through the doorway. It was making straight for him—worse than that, it was, horribly, going clammily through him, streaming into ragged ribbons of mist and round into a whirlwind to surround the frail figure of the old man.

Tarq, in the middle of the storm, was still and calm. Nian backed as far away from the swirling mists as he could. This old man could call on so much power: enough to snuff Nian out like a candle. *I hate him*, Nian thought, as fiercely as he could.

Tarq was looking pale, now, almost as if he were fading—but before Nian could be quite sure whether this was any more than an effect of the mists, the scent of hot water was jerking his attention away to the pool.

And it was *steaming*.

To swim in *warm* water was a luxury beyond Nian's imagining. He dipped in a cautious toe. The water was

21

much warmer than the air in that great chilly cavern of a room. He slid in and pushed himself across the pool. The floor of the pool was decorated with a pattern of interlocking spiked circles that was echoed in the carving on the domes above his head.

I hate this place, he thought. *I must escape.*

But the thoughts floated away from him into the water, somehow, as if they weren't important.

Nian shook his head to clear it. *I hate this place*, he thought again, more fiercely. But still the words didn't bite in his mind.

A idea drifted by him, as if on the water: *I'm dissolving*, he thought, and the terror of that cleared his brain completely.

I'm Nian, he thought, *and I'm going to escape.*

At once he was aware again of the hot-iron scent of the power of the House. It'd been there all the time, of course, but the power of those smothering swathes of fleeces had been leaching his will away, and quickly, quickly. Every breath he took was smoothing away his anger, his scorn, his will. Nian turned round in the gently steaming pool and his heart quailed at the knowledge that, quietly but relentlessly, he was being destroyed.

I can't die, he told himself. *It's too soon. And I have to go home.*

But he was losing track of the hot-iron power again already, and he panicked so completely that he even lost control of the screen in his mind that normally shuttered off his special powers. The screen snapped

22

open, and suddenly he couldn't breathe at all. There was layer upon layer of tepid invisible fleece pressed around his mouth and nostrils. He squirmed over in panic and dived down to the bottom of the pool where the swathes of fleece couldn't follow him. He crouched there, shivering despite the warmth, until he could bear it no longer and he was forced to boost himself up so his nose cleared the water. But it was still impossible to breathe, for the soft curds of the fleeces were clinging to the surface like foam.

But they weren't really there, he told himself fiercely, desperately. Tarq had talked about powers of the mind, so these horrible things were only *thought* there. So he must *think* of a way of protecting himself.

His lungs were aching, but he tried to call to mind something, something like an extra skin, that would cover him. He imagined it as hard as he could— and to his colossal relief he felt something settling over him.

But he still couldn't breathe, and at that he panicked again, so badly he only just had the presence of mind to imagine the skin pierced by many tiny holes, large enough to let air through, but small enough to keep out the smothering power of the House. A prickling wave swept smartingly over him from his head to his feet, but before it was finished he was heaving in lungful after lungful of clean air, and floating, limp as a leaf, under the white spike-carved domes.

When his breathing had calmed down he tested out the protecting skin by calling up a picture of home.

And he was so wrenched by the loss of it that he would have climbed out of the pool and run away there and then, except that Tarq was standing by the door.

'That's good,' said Tarq, when Nian had shrugged on the pale green tunic and leggings of the uniform that Tarq had brought him. 'I shall make your hair grow long enough to plait and then you'll be quite fit for the House. Now come. You must meet the other pupils.'

The House was so quiet that it hardly seemed possible there could be any others, but Nian only needed there to be one nice stupid friendly boy who could explain the routine of the House. That would be enough for Nian to plan his escape.

There were actually two boys in the room to which Tarq led him, but neither of them looked either stupid or friendly. They were both older than Nian. One of them, an absent-minded, rather heron-like youth of about seventeen, was so thin he seemed little more than a column of balanced bones, and the other, a broad-shouldered boy a couple of years younger, had a wary, belligerent look in his dark eyes that promised trouble.

Nian turned to Tarq.

'Where are the other pupils?' he asked.

'There are no others,' answered Tarq, sadly. 'Gifted boys are rare, and are becoming rarer. But still, it is foretold that the Lords will become fewer as the time of the Truth Sayer approaches, so that itself is a sign of hope. Caul, here, came six years ago, and soon he will become a Lord of Truth. Varn has been here only two years, but he is already strong in Wisdom—as you will be too, soon, my son.'

Varn's lips curled incredulously, and Nian discovered that he disliked Varn very much.

'You will eat and sleep, now,' Tarq went on. 'I shall return at dawn and then you will begin your training.'

If I'm still here, Nian told himself, as the old man's footsteps faded away along the endless stone floor of the corridor.

2

Jacob paused outside his bedroom door. There was a rapid drumming coming from inside the room, but experience told him that this time it had nothing to do with bongoes.

He pushed open the door cautiously.

Robyn was lying on her bottom bunk, and she was punching her pillow as hard and as fast as she could. This was actually a fairly good sign: at least she was punching the *pillow*.

Jacob tiptoed across the lino to where he'd left his football. The room was only eight feet long, so getting in and out should only have been the work of seconds; it *would* have been, if someone hadn't left Jacob's jumper on the floor. Well, the jumper hardly slowed him down at all, but the hairbrush underneath it nearly crippled him.

'Ooooowwww!' he yelled, clutching a foot that had been stabbed by a hundred vicious spikes.

Robyn kicked out at him. It was only a random, irritable sort of kick, but Jacob, off-balance, fell against the wardrobe, got his feet tangled up in the bin, and somehow found himself mummified inside a long tube of curtain.

'*LEAVE ME ALONE!!!!*' yelled Robyn.

Jacob waited for his ears to stop ringing, and then he extricated himself. 'Sorry,' he said.

Robyn's teeth were bared and her dark hair was standing up on end. Both of these were *bad* signs.

'*Why* do I have to be stuck with you?' she snarled. 'Why can't I just get some *peace and quiet*?'

Not for the first time, Jacob was grateful Robyn couldn't hear the *Wherever* noises in the front room. It seemed to be from some sort of quarry at the moment: there were lots of gears changing, and sometimes a gravel-tipping sort of roar. Jacob would have been quite interested to see it.

'I'm just going away,' he said, quite reasonably, he thought. But Robyn thumped her pillow even harder.

'Yes, but you'll come back!' she snapped.

Experience told Jacob there wasn't going to be anything very much he could say to help.

'*I can't stand it any longer,*' said Robyn, in a sort of crazed growl. 'I'm not asking for much. I can cope with the fact that everyone hates me because I'm still wearing boot-cut jeans. I can even cope with the fact that Nan's taste in interior design hasn't changed since World War Two. All I want,' she went on, slightly brokenly, 'all I want is to sit down quietly and design my room that I haven't got. IS THAT SO MUCH TO ASK?'

'Right, yeah,' said Jacob. 'I mean no,' he added, hastily, twitching away from a glare that could have stripped the paint off the wall. 'Of course not.'

'Nan's always nagging me to do something moronically domestic!' Robyn went on. 'There I am, trying to be *creative*, and she wants me *to hang the washing up*!'

'Yeah,' said Jacob. 'But, hey, keep your voice down a bit, Rob, OK?'

Robyn took a deep breath . . . and held it. When she did speak, it was more quietly, but with huge intensity of feeling.

'And *Dad* sits there with a towel over his head, inhaling ylang-ylang,' she said, bitterly. 'And of course *Mum* takes sides with Nan.'

Jacob felt a sudden pang of extreme sympathy for his mother. Jacob didn't go in for planning, much, but he made a point of not getting between Nan and Robyn if he could help it: the smallest sign of trouble and he was *out* of there. But Mum would throw herself between them quite recklessly, like a mouse trying to separate a pair of bulldogs.

'I'm going up to the park to have a kick-around,' said Jacob. 'Fancy coming?'

Robyn made an odd noise like a sneezing peke.

'Just *leave me alone*!'

'Yeah, fine. See you later, then!'

Jacob ran down the stairs, being careful to tread lightly so as not to wear out Nan's stair carpet. The people at the quarry in the front room *Wherever* seemed to be having a tea-break.

He'd forgotten all of them before he'd even got to the front gate.

There was no point in worrying.

Varn surveyed Nian critically. 'You're all I need,' he said. 'A babysitting job.' Nian made an effort and decided not to punch Varn's teeth in.

'I'm Nian,' he said.

'Are you?' said Varn, with absolutely no interest. 'Well, just stand over there, *Nian*, and shut up. I've got work to do.'

Varn went and sat down cross-legged in an arched alcove. He stretched his back very straight, held up his arms as Tarq had done over the pool, and closed his eyes. Nothing happened for several seconds, but then, just as Tarq had done, he began to look somehow misty and far away.

He snapped back into full colour almost at once.

'There,' he announced, a little short of breath, but really much too pleased with himself. 'Dinner is served.'

Nian looked, and looked again. There were three wooden bowls on the floor in the corner that had surely not been there before.

Nian made the effort to brush away all feelings of respect and interest and then he caught the smell of the bowls and stopped being impressed at once.

'Porridge,' he said, in dismay.

Varn shot him a very sharp look.

'Your mind should be on higher things, Nian. All right. See if you can manage your first duty. Take Caul his bowl.'

Caul took the bowl automatically, without his eyes ever seeming to focus on anything. Varn was already scooping up glistening dollops of grey gunge as if he were starving, so Nian picked up the last bowl. The stuff tasted as good as it looked—not good at all—but the worst thing was that there wasn't nearly enough of it. By the time Nian had finished scraping round his bowl there was no need to wash it.

'I shall take the bowls back to the scullery,' announced Varn. 'You stay here. Don't touch anything.'

But there was a little porridge left in in the bottom of Caul's bowl, and Nian needed that food, for he had a long journey ahead of him.

'I'll take them, Varn,' he said, as humbly as he could. 'It isn't right that you should wait on me. Not when you're older than me, and so clever.'

Varn gave him another razor-sharp look. Then he got to his feet.

'Get Caul's bowl, then,' he ordered. 'And I'll show you where to go.'

Fifty paces down the chilly corridor there was a room containing a stone trough. Varn led Nian in, closed the huge pale door, and put his back to it.

'You've shielded yourself from the power of the House,' he said.

Nian wondered for a wild moment whether he could pretend not to understand, but Varn's dark eyes were sharp and clever.

Then Nian realized something else.

'And so have you,' he said, with sudden, dawning hope.

Varn hurled his bowl across the room, strode forward two steps, and grabbed Nian by the collar of his tunic. Varn was strong, and all Nian could do was wince away as the bowl clattered and bounced to a stop.

'All right,' said Varn, fiercely, shaking him. 'We're both protected but if you dare breathe a word of this to anyone I'll break every bone in your body. Understand?'

Nian tried to answer, but his tunic was strangling him and he couldn't speak.

'You little *cretin*!' Varn snarled. 'Why did *you* have to turn up!'

Nian managed to say something.

'The Tarhun kidnapped me,' he gulped.

Varn pushed him away in disgust.

'You little, moronic, stupid, *blithering* idiot,' he growled. '*The Tarhun kidnapped me?* How obviously free of the power can you get?'

'I don't know,' said Nian, tenderly checking that his head was still attached to his body. 'I've only just got here. Why does it matter so much?'

'Because, you little fool, if Tarq finds out you're free, he'll destroy your shield—he could do that in a minute—and then he'd wonder about me—and that'd be the end of any chance I've got of getting out of here.' Varn's dark eyes went remote. 'The end of *me*, pretty much. I'd be here for ever. *For ever.*'

Nian turned his head experimentally. There were only minor amounts of clicking and graunching.

'So how are you going to escape?' he asked.

Varn turned on him, snarling, and Nian hastily put the trough between them. Then Varn gave a great sigh.

'Oh, I suppose I'll have to tell you, you pathetic little runt. But we'll put away these left-overs first. Give me that bowl.'

'My name's Nian.'

'Little *Nian*, then.'

Nian watched hungrily as Varn shared out the remains of the porridge. One portion was probably larger than the other, but it was pretty nearly fair, especially when you considered that Varn was bigger than Nian was, and that until today he'd been able to scoff the lot.

But even with the left-overs from the dozen bowls that were stacked by the trough there wasn't nearly enough to eat.

'Do you know how to wash up?' demanded Varn, when they'd finished.

'Of course I do!'

'All right. Then get on with it.'

Nian hesitated, but he could still feel Varn's grasp round his neck. Nian found a frayed stick by the trough and began to scrub the bowls. Varn stood glowering over him for a few minutes, but then he took up a drying rag.

'Look,' said Varn, at last, but not quite so fiercely. 'You've got to understand that we're both in really desperate danger. You've felt the power of the House; you know what it does.'

Nian shivered as he remembered.

'It stops you thinking what you want to think,' he said.

Varn smiled very grimly.

'Oh, that's not the half of it,' he said. 'Tarq and the Lords . . . they're all completely mad, but their powers are colossal. We can't begin to fight them. Do you understand?'

Nian nodded. There were things in this place so vast that he didn't even dare think about them.

'Our only chance,' went on Varn, 'is that they carry on thinking we're under the House's power. So we have to act as if we're in a dream all the time. That's what the power of the House does, you see: it makes real things seem shadowy, and their powers, what the Lords call their *Wisdom*, solid and real.'

Nian gave one of the bowls an extra hard scrubbing.

'This Wisdom,' he said, 'is it the same sort of thing as the powers I have?'

'Yes, but about a thousand times stronger. It's like I used to summon supper. It's more difficult to get it to work when you haven't got the power of the House to call on, so you'll have to concentrate as hard on your lessons as you possibly can.'

Nian remembered the suffocating fleeces that thickened the air. He shuddered with disgust.

'And, Nian,' Varn went on, 'if you cause any trouble at all—if you give Tarq or any of the others any reason to doubt for one moment that you're under the control of the House—I'll give you the biggest going-over you've ever had.'

He meant it.

Nian shook the water from the last bowl.

'All right,' said Varn. 'I'll take you to where we sleep.'

High up in one white wall of the sleeping room there was an opening about two spans' depth and four across. It was hardly big enough to be called a window, but through it blew the soft scent of growing things, and the sight of the heart-shaped leaves of the holm-tree that rose sharp against the magenta of the evening sky gave Nian such a sharp wrench of homesickness that he could have howled.

'Where's the door to the outside?' he asked.

'I'm not telling you,' answered Varn, shortly. 'That's the garden, and only the Lords are allowed to go in, and then only on special days after lots of fasting and stuff. It's sort of holy, because it's where our world touches the others.'

'But I can't stay inside all the time!' exclaimed Nian, ignoring this crazy talk of other worlds, because the thought of being inside any longer gave him a tight, desperate feeling as if his insides were shrivelling. 'Give me a back up,' he said pleadingly. 'I won't be long. And I expect I'll be able to get back in all right. I'm good at climbing.'

Varn turned on him in exasperation.

'You *expect*?' he echoed. 'And what if you can't? Don't you get it? If you're under the power of the House then you *don't break rules*. If anyone saw you out there that'd be the end for both of us. The *end*, do you understand? The Lords would search you until they found out the truth of you, and they'd use it to destroy all the bits of you that weren't theirs.'

Nian made an effort and pushed the desperate feeling away. It left him feeling very empty, somehow.

'It's just that I come from a farm,' he said. 'And I'm not inside all that much, usually.'

Varn heaved an impatient sigh.

'Yes, all right, I know,' he said. 'My father's a silk merchant, and if you knew how I long to smell silk again, or to hear scissors cutting cloth—oh, I want to punch holes in the walls, sometimes. But if we give the game away we'll never get out. Never. So we've got to be very careful, and we've got to be patient. Got it?'

'I suppose so.'

'You'd better have done,' said Varn.

Varn unrolled a sleeping mat along the floor and threw another one at Nian. It smelt of mould and dead spiders.

'So how *are* you going to escape?' Nian asked again, as he fumbled at the strange fastenings of his tunic.

Varn checked the door so fast he nearly took off.

'Keep your voice *down*!' he hissed. Then he sighed. 'Don't you realize, you total *imbecile*, that if anyone had heard what you'd just said that would have finished us? You can't hear the Lords coming, you know, half the time. They're like cats.'

'Sorry,' said Nian. Varn glared at him.

'I'd be better off smothering you,' he said, darkly. 'All right. Listen. I've been here for two years. I've explored the whole place and checked out everything, and you can't get out. Not in any ordinary way, anyway. I was beginning to think I was stuck here for ever, but then I found something in the library. They've got centuries of stuff written down in there.'

'And . . . can you read it?' asked Nian.

'Of course I can read it,' snapped Varn; Nian had to struggle not to be impressed. He knew that some very learned people could tell each other wise things by making signs on rolls of hartskin, but obviously it must be a terribly terribly difficult thing to do.

'Lots of the stuff in there hasn't been touched for hundreds of years,' went on Varn. 'And I found something important.'

'What?'

A glint of triumph lit up Varn's dark eyes.

'How to *fly*,' he said.

Nian's careful scepticism vanished like smoke. Varn had been talking about powers, but this was something useful. Something *desirable*.

'But . . . can you really do it?' he asked, in a whisper.

'A bit. But it's difficult. I practise every day, but I reckon it'll be another whole year before I'll be able to get over the wall.'

A year? Nian's interest vanished. He wasn't staying in this place for a year.

'Why can't you just climb out?' he demanded.

'Because, bird-brain, there's a sort of power-net thing along the wall that stops you. I read about that in the library, too.'

Nian settled himself down on his sleeping mat. If it was going to take Varn a whole year to learn to fly, then it would probably take Nian until doomsday. But that didn't mean he was stuck here. He was small, so he might be able to wriggle through one of the holes in that power-net and climb over the roofs of the Outer House and away. Why, Varn said the scrolls were very old, so the net might quite likely have rotted to pieces, or been nibbled by bush-rats.

He could try, anyway. He *would* try. If he set out at night, secretly, then no one would know. It could do no harm.

It was cold, so Nian pulled his cover over him and settled down. His mat smelt wrong: not of Grandy and soapwort, but of mildew and hot irons and danger.

He began thinking carefully about the climb, but somehow it kept getting muddled up with the Tarhun, and new bread and ground-finches . . .

He dreamed of home.

3

There were sounds of fighting coming from the front room today. This *Wherever* wasn't all that loud, really, but there was definitely bellowing, and the clashing of swords.

Quite a big battle, experience told Jacob, and quite likely to go on through tomorrow, as well.

Nan came shuffling along the hall in answer to the doorbell.

'Mind out of the way, then,' she muttered. 'Haven't you got anything better to do than hang about making the place look untidy?'

'Well . . . not really,' said Jacob.

Nan threw him a sour look.

'A great lout like you,' she said. 'I had a job in a shop at your age. *And* I gave some of my pay packet to my mother.'

Jacob wondered about explaining that he was too young to get a job in a shop, but decided against it. He would actually have quite liked a job: the money would certainly have come in useful, what with Dad not be able to go to work.

'Ooh, my stomach's playing up,' said Nan. 'I don't

know what your mother put in that dinner last night. Let me get to the door, then.'

Jacob would have gone away, but Nan was blocking off the bottom of the stairs, Dad was in the kitchen doing a bit of Chilean head massage, and Robyn was busy in the back room designing a chest of drawers.

'Ah,' said Nan, opening the door. 'Violet. How nice you could come.'

'Hello, Mrs Hinde,' said Jacob, politely, to the little old lady who blinked anxiously at him from the door-mat. He hoped that Mrs Hinde, like Nan, couldn't hear the noises in the front room, because it sounded very much as though someone had just been killed; this would be bound to put a bit of a dampener on her afternoon tea, even though Mum had made them a fruit cake before she left for work.

Mind you, the front room was weird, anyway. Nan had the place so full of ornaments that there were always about a hundred china eyes staring at you. In fact, almost the only thing in the place *without* eyes was the chunk of old rock on the mantelpiece that Grandad had brought back from holiday once—mostly, Jacob suspected, in protest at all the ornaments.

'Don't mind the boy,' said Nan. 'He's just going out.'

Jacob gave up on his plan to go up to his room and read through *Total Drumming* again: he'd have a wander up to the shop and perhaps buy himself something to eat, instead.

No worries.

$\cancel{||||} |$

At home, the day pretty much began with breakfast. In the House of Truth it began with all the Lords and their pupils shuffling in a silent procession to the Council Chamber for the first hour of Wisdom.

This involved sitting *completely still* for a *whole hour*.

Everybody sat with closed eyes and dead expressions, and everybody but Nian seemed oblivious to the hardness of the stone floor that struck up freezingly through the mats. There were twelve Lords—just twelve—and though some of them were younger than that one over there who looked like a mummified tortoise, they were none of them anything near young.

After this hilarious procedure everyone shuffled off and ate more porridge. Nian tried to talk to Varn, but Varn would hardly look at him.

After breakfast Varn led him to the schoolroom. Tarq was waiting for them, his face split in a horrible flensed-carcass smile.

'Welcome, my son Nian, to the beginning of your studies,' he said. 'Your work will be hard, but any

suffering will be as nothing compared with the great-
ness of our purpose. Now, come here.'

Tarq began to teach Nian to read that day. Nian,
with Varn's sharp eyes on him, listened carefully, and
was amazed at how simple it was.

'You're another like Varn,' Tarq remarked, at last.
'Quick-witted, and restless to learn.'

Nian could not help but be a little pleased.

The morning's study was followed by dinner
(bread) which was followed by the second hour of
Wisdom, more study, the third hour of Wisdom, bathe
in the pool, supper—and bed. Nian found the sitting
and studying annoying enough, but the sitting round
gazing into space drove him to screaming point.

'What on earth's the *point* of it all?' he asked Varn,
irritably, as they washed up. To Nian's relief, Varn had
snapped back into being his normal self once the last
hour of Wisdom had finished.

'It helps to focus your powers.'

'And what's the point of *them*?' snapped Nian, for he
felt as if he had never in his life spent such a useless day.

Varn shrugged.

'Powers—Wisdom—it discovers the truth about
things. You have to do that before you can control them.
The Lords can do all sorts of stuff: govern the weather,
or the pool, or cure a sickness. They can, you know; you
won't be ill much while you're in here. And the Lords
keep our world safe from the others, of course.'

Nian frowned.

'The other what?'

'The other worlds.'

Nian looked sideways at him, but Varn didn't look as if he were messing about.

'But there aren't any other worlds,' he pointed out, 'that's stories.'

'Yes,' agreed Varn, impatiently. 'True stories.'

'But how do you know . . . ?'

'Oh good grief,' said Varn. 'Don't you know *anything*?'

Nian knew many things: how to grow lace-parsley; how to milk a hind; about the blustery wind that would pass through the valleys tomorrow.

'Not about other worlds,' he said.

Varn heaved a sigh.

'Oh, blast you for an ignoramus. There was an invasion, wasn't there. Centuries ago. Before this House was built. There was a big earthquake, and then a whole bunch of warriors appeared where the garden is now. Well, naturally everyone ran screaming, except the Lords, who called up their Wisdom and sort of misted up the warriors' minds and made them run away back to their own world.'

Nian was intrigued, but disappointed. It would have been a better story if the Lords had made the warriors' heads explode, or turned them all to ice and shattered them with mallets.

'And they've never come back?' he said, regretfully.

'If you got out of here, would *you* come back?'

Varn's tone was withering, but Nian was fascinated by the idea of another world.

'How did the warriors get here?' he asked, imagining

a cart, and then a boat, and then an eagle, and then dismissing them all as impossible.

'No one knows, but people think that the earthquake might have broken something. The worlds turn beside each other, you see: it's like the patterns in the pool chamber. You'll read about it later. Or . . . have you ever seen the insides of a clock?'

Nian shook his head: he'd never seen a clock at all. What was the use of a clock, when the suns told the time so gloriously?

'Yokel,' said Varn, in disgust. 'Well, imagine wheels with little spikes sticking out all round them.'

Nian imagined it.

'Right, now imagine them brought together so the spikes fit between each other. That means that if one circle turns then the others will turn, too, because the spikes will push each other round. The worlds are like that, you see, actually touching each other. The Lords' Wisdom makes a barrier round our world to protect it from another world breaking through. That's really why this place is important.'

Nian looked round at the solid stone walls. It was hard to believe that the world was so fragile.

'Do you understand, now, little Nian?'

'Sort of.'

'Good,' said Varn, sitting himself down on the floor. 'So now shut up. I need to concentrate.'

Nian was ready to scream at the thought of shutting up. The silence of the House pressed in on him. He didn't mind not talking, for when he was at work in the fields he often went hours without exchanging a word with anyone. But at home there were always birds singing, and the companionship of the evening to look forward to. And the food.

Nian remembered the rich brown stock-pot that bubbled constantly above the kitchen fire, and he suddenly knew that he had to escape at once, that night, and never mind what Varn had said. He'd climb the wall and get out. He'd run and run, for if he was headed home then surely he could run for ever. And if the Tarhun came after him he would crush their heads with boulders, trip them down ravines, poison them with darkshade.

Nian gave Varn a sideways glance . . . and promptly forgot everything else.

Varn was still sitting cross-legged, but he wasn't sitting *on* anything: he was hovering a foot off the floor.

Nian's mouth fell open. Streamers of fierce power were whirling round Varn, keeping him in the air.

Nian had known Varn was strong, but this was amazing, terrifying, tingling . . .

. . . and the tingling had got up Nian's nose before he knew it. He sneezed, loudly and violently, and at once beside him there was a horrible *thud*, and then a cry of pain and outrage.

Nian hardly dared open his eyes. Varn was on his back on the floor, staring up wildly at the ceiling.

Then Varn took two deep breaths and said a word that probably hadn't been heard in the House for a thousand years.

'It was an accident,' said Nian, pleadingly, as Varn began to get up. 'I couldn't help it.'

Nian tried to dodge, but Varn had long arms and he was between Nian and the door. Varn thumped Nian really quite hard. Nian, rubbing himself ruefully, reckoned they were about quits, but Varn didn't seem to think so. They got ready for bed in as cold and perfect a silence as any in that House.

✝✝ ‖

The lesser sun had followed the greater down behind
the glassy green rocks of the mountains, and now the
sky was glowing with the stars.

Nian untangled himself very carefully from his cover
and snatched at his clothes. His breath sounded loud
in the freezing silence of the House.

He looked at the two dark hummocks that were
all he could see of the others. Varn was snoring, but
Caul . . . he'd have to risk Caul. Anyway, Caul was so
dopey that he'd hardly notice if a band of prancing
Sirrom men tried to stick their bells up his nose. Nian
gathered up his courage and took a first cautious step
into the darkness. Everything was quiet—but then
everything was always quiet. For all he knew he could
be surrounded by a dozen watching figures.

Nian made his way anxiously, one step at a time.
Outside the sleeping room door everything was utterly
black. What if he blundered into one of the Lords'
rooms? Or into a pile of prayer-dishes?

Nian was so used to keeping his powers behind the
screen in his mind that it hardly ever occurred to him
to use them, but now, faced with this blackness, he

tried raising the screen a little, and at once the blackness around him squirmed and seemed to come alive. This was such a shock that it panicked him for a moment, but then, gradually, he raised the screen altogether and looked around using all his powers.

It was confusing—like having two sets of eyes and ears that told you different things. For one thing, though it was dark, he could tell where everything was, and again, though he could hear the silence, he could somehow also hear the minds of the men in the House . . . not distinctly, but with a vague impression of colour. He looked at one of the blurs and it came sharply into focus and showed a woman sitting sewing by a fire. That could have been anyone's dream, so he looked at another one and this time he saw a picture of himself bending over a scroll. That must be Tarq's mind, he realized, with an uneasy pang of guilt; after that he didn't look any more.

He stepped forward watchfully. There were heavy power-fleeces everywhere, but he could find his way, now. He slipped out of the pupils' rooms and into the wide corridor. A hundred paces or so to his left was the great door. He heaved at the handle and it eased open to reveal, blue in the moonlight, the path that led to the Outer House.

Nian had a sharp inner conviction that this was too easy, but he brushed it aside and slipped through into the night.

His extra senses dimmed a little when he stepped over the threshold of the House, but he could still

47

make out the minds of the Lords behind him, and, blunter but greedier, those of the Tarhun in front. The moon was rising over the wall of the Outer House: it was new, and cast little light, but it seemed the most ravishingly beautiful thing after being imprisoned inside for so many hours; the slender mirror-crescents were so taut he almost seemed to hear them humming.

The door at the other end of the path was lost in darkness. Nian stepped off the path and into the shadow of the wall. He could make out the first few feet of wall fairly well. The stone blocks had the occasional crumbled edge that would provide holds for a climb. If he ran out, he would have to climb back down and try somewhere else, that was all.

If he could.

Nian had been climbing almost before he could walk. The family told rueful tales of discovering him on high shelves, on roofs, even, where it was surely impossible for a year-old baby to be. Miri had once rescued him from the rafters above the bull's stall, and Grandy often talked about the relief, when Tan came along, of having a baby that actually stayed where it was put. Nian had vague strange memories of that time: of being frustrated, angry; he had a muddled idea that those feelings had somehow helped boost him upwards, away from the annoying world.

But they couldn't be real memories, he'd always told himself, but without quite believing it.

The first part of the climb was no harder than climbing the hay barn at home, except that the stone struck cold into his fingers.

He moved slowly, and with great care, for there were Tarhun on the other side of the wall; it was lucky he did, for as he reached up to a new hold his hand banged into something hard. Something hard, but completely invisible.

He withdrew his hand and tried again. There was certainly nothing there—but at the same time the obstacle, whatever it was, was as solid as the stone of the wall itself. He squinted up, focusing his powers carefully, and found he could sense a lattice of thick rope-like stuff that stretched along the wall. Yes, Varn had told him about this: it was a net, a power-net.

Nian, spread-eagled against the cold stone of the wall, leaned back as far as he dared and squinted upwards. The gaps between the ropes were a couple of spans wide—perhaps wide enough for him to squeeze through. He'd try, in any case.

It took a lot of courage to trust his weight to the invisible strands of the net. He got a good hold of one of them, then groped about for a heart-jerking couple of seconds and found another.

He paused there for a moment, clutching as hard as he could at nothing, preparing himself for the next effort.

He drew in a deep breath, and quickly, neatly, pulled himself upwards.

His scalp tingled as his head came up through the gap between the strands of netting, but he managed to hook an armpit over an invisible rope. That felt ever so much safer. He hooked his other arm over and hung for a moment.

The effort had made him go a bit dizzy, but he ignored this and peered up, searching for more barriers. All he could sense above him were the stars and the crescents of the moon.

He felt a rush of triumph. He could climb anything, so there was nothing to worry about any more . . .

. . . except that the stars were *moving*.

They really were: they were twisting, slowly, into spirals. Yes, and now they were spinning faster, and beside them the silver crescents of the moon were accelerating into a spiky circle.

Nian, giddy, closed his eyes, but the whirling had spun right into his mind and now his thoughts were melting, bending, twisting, curling up on themselves until Nian was no longer even sure who he was, or where he was, and it was all he could do to keep his arms braced over the net.

Varn had been right: this power, this Wisdom, was terrifying. Nian's brain was warping, bleaching, as though every one of his thoughts was being laid out, and equalled, and neutralized.

He had to get out of this net and back to the wall. And quickly, quickly, for he was turning into a whirlpool and spinning round, down, downwards . . .

. . . he tried to focus his eyes on something solid, but the whole world was spinning, now, waltzing and lurching round him. Even the wall seemed to be caving into the great whirlpool that was whirling round him, through him, round and round and round and . . .

He took a gulping breath, but his muscles were melting, too, now, like his mind, and even that was too much.

He fell for a long desperate second. Then he thumped into the ground, and everything splintered into writhing sparks of agony.

And then—nothing.

4

'The thing is, Sue, that I think I might be getting a bit depressed,' said Dad.

'Again? Oh, how awful,' said Mum, with feeling.

'I had a long talk about it with Blossom—you know, the one in the Health Food Shop—'

'Yes, I know. The one who always wears the hand-woven poncho and wellies.'

'—that's right. It's just that I get low, sometimes, when I'm stuck in here all day while you're out at the café.'

'I know,' said Mum. 'I know.'

'*Susan!*'

Mum smiled bravely at Nan's nose, which had appeared round the door.

'Yes, Mum?'

'Have you done the hoovering yet? Because I want to have my nap.'

'Yes, yes, it's all right. I did it while you were in town.'

'And did you put the bins out?'

'Oh, I'll do that as soon as I've finished my cuppa.'

'Only you never know when the men are coming.'

'And as I was saying to Blossom—'

'I'll put the bins out,' offered Jacob. 'Then you can listen to Dad.'

'Oh, would you really? Oh, that is nice of you, Jacob. Thank you.'

Jacob went off whistling. It was no trouble, and it got him away from the *Wherever* sounds of the herds of wildebeest or whatever crossing the plains. It was important to keep Nan happy, or else she might throw them out of her house and then they'd probably have to go to live across town in the muggers' district.

The sound of Dad's worrying died away as Jacob went out through the kitchen. And that was good, too.

$$\text{卌 |||}$$

Nian hurt. That was all he knew, except for a vague feeling that he was being moved. It hurt so much he couldn't bear to be awake; so he let everything black out again.

Now someone was splashing icy water in his face. Nian turned his head away and made the huge effort to haul up a groan of protest. He was still in an enormous amount of pain. It was dark, but he could just see the high-up oblong of window that told him he was in the sleeping room. That was the wrong . . . the wrong . . . the *wrong place*—but he was too confused to know exactly why.

'*Nian!*'

Someone was saying his name in a tiny whisper that somehow clanged around his skull as loudly as the welcoming bell.

'*Nian!*'

Nian managed to say something, though he didn't know what.

'*Are you all right?*'

Nian groaned—not with pain, exactly, but with the stupidity of the question.

'Where does it hurt?' asked the voice, anxiously. 'Can you move your fingers and toes?'

Nian lay still for a moment, trying to work out who this was, who he was, why he was supposed to move.

'Try,' said the voice. 'Go on, Nian: please try.'

Nian sighed—and then winced, for that hurt very much. Yes, the pain worsened every time he took a breath.

Alarmed, now, he did try moving his fingers and toes. They seemed to work.

'No limbs broken,' said the voice, jerky with relief. 'Thank goodness for that, you complete, moronic, *cretinous* little idiot! Can you turn your head?'

Nian tried. That hurt, too, but it felt like an ache, not a wound. He felt oddly alone, somehow, like a fish cast up on a river bank. He made the great effort to speak.

'Who are you?' he asked.

'It's Varn,' the voice answered, more shaken still. 'You remember me.'

Nian let his memory take him from his home until his arrival in the place where *Varn* was. Yes, he remembered. He was in the House of Truth, and he had failed to escape. He was in the House of Truth and he had failed. He was in the House of Truth.

'I remember,' he whispered; if he'd been younger he might have cried.

'We must be careful not to wake Caul up,' came Varn's voice from the darkness beside him. 'I've put a dome of silence over him, but it's not perfect. Do you think you're badly hurt?'

Nian took in just enough air to reply.

'It hurts when I breathe,' he whispered.

Varn hissed.

'You're lucky to have got off as lightly as that,' he said bitterly. 'You could have broken your neck. And after I *told* you about that power-net! You're lucky you haven't broken both your legs, and your back to go with them.'

Nian lay still and took short shallow breaths.

'It really hurts,' he whispered.

'Good,' said Varn. 'If it hadn't, little Nian, I'd have given you the biggest going-over you've ever had in your life . . . What on *earth* are we going to say to Tarq?'

But Nian couldn't begin to work that out. The pain was taking up too much of his mind.

'We'll have to say you fell over,' went on Varn, gloomily. 'That's true, too, sort of. Honestly, and after I *explained* to you it's vital the Lords don't realize we're shielded from the power of the House! What if I hadn't heard your mind scream as you fell? That would have been a bit of a giveaway, wouldn't it, the Lords finding you underneath the Outer Wall?'

It hurt. Nian thought about the hours and hours until daylight and he wasn't sure he could exist through them. He needed someone to come and look after him. He needed someone who'd stop the pain. Grandy had a potion that was good for pain.

But Grandy was far away.

'Varn . . . please . . . ' he whispered.

Through the darkness he was somehow aware of Varn staring at him.

'What?' he demanded.

But Nian didn't have the strength to work out what. He lay, breathing shallow, painful breaths.

Varn said the word he'd said earlier, when he'd fallen out of his levitation.

'All right,' he said crossly. 'All right, I'll go and get Tarq. And Grodan, I suppose, he's the most powerful healer in the House. Stay there,' he went on, unnecessarily. 'I'll make up some story. Sleep-walking. Yes, that'll have to do. And don't you dare contradict it, or I'll break every other bone in your body.'

Nian thought a lot while he waited for Tarq and Grodan to come. The pain was the main thing, but there was home, as well, and the fertile valleys that lay cupped within the mountains. And then there was the power-net. The net changed everything. He couldn't get past it, and that meant he couldn't escape by climbing the wall.

And that meant he couldn't escape.

̶H̶H̶ ||||

The broken ends of Nian's ribs were fused together by the Lords' powers of Wisdom. Varn secretly moved Nian's protective skin deeper into Nian's chest on the wounded side, and at least one of the Lords sat impassively beside Nian for two whole days, by which time the bones were encased in a hard substance that held them together perfectly. Nian was grateful, and he even wished his powers were as strong as the Lords', but he never for a moment doubted that the valleys were where he belonged.

'Where would you have gone if you *had* escaped?' asked Varn, one evening. And as Nian opened his mouth to say *home*, he realized that home would have been the first place the Tarhun would have looked for him. Whatever happened, he could not go home.

'Where will *you* go?' Nian asked in his turn.

'Oh, a big city. Somewhere I can go about without being noticed. I'll get a job with a cloth merchant, I expect. I know all about that.'

It sounded very dull. But it was true that in the valleys every stranger was big news. The Tarhun would be bound to hear about any newcomer.

'I don't think I'll be able to go anywhere I really want to be,' Nian said at last.

'Well, then, let down your shield so the power of the House can take you over. You'll be content, then.'

But Nian shook his head. He couldn't do that. That would be like killing himself. And while he was in his own mind then there must be a little hope.

'All right,' said Varn. 'In that case you'd better start thinking about learning to fly.'

From that moment Nian flung himself into his studies with every ounce of energy he possessed. Varn was older than he was, and had been studying for two whole years, but Nian was determined to catch him up. If Nian was left in the House after Varn had gone then the Lords would turn on him and strip him of his shield—and that would be the end of him.

Nian made rapid progress. Before a month was out he was reading quite fluently, and in another month he had access to enough power to make the water in the pool so hot that neither Varn nor he could get in it. On that occasion Tarq, who had been looking increasingly thoughtful, called Nian aside to remonstrate.

'My son,' he said gravely, 'you must not be so intemperate. The powers that you have are precious and rare, and you must use them judiciously. They are given to you, but they are not yours to waste. They are for the good of all the Lords.'

'It was an accident,' explained Nian, apologetically.

Tarq frowned, which was the severest punishment he ever inflicted on any of his pupils.

'That is surely hardly possible,' he said. 'You must have known when the water was warm enough, my son. You could have turned aside your power then.'

'No,' said Nian, for he was quite upset about it himself, because he and Varn had narrowly missed scalding themselves badly. 'My power came on in a sort of surge,' he explained, hesitatingly. 'By the time I'd worked out how to stop it, it was too late.'

Tarq opened his mouth but then he closed it again while he considered what to say.

'My son,' said Tarq, at last, with a smile that was almost rueful, 'I think that perhaps for now you had better leave the heating of the pool to Varn. And tomorrow we will draw our attention to the control of your gifts.'

Nian really tried, but he was hopeless. He couldn't control his powers at all. The first, basic, exercise involved levitating a bowl of water from one part of the floor to another. Tarq could move the bowl in a graceful arc so that not one drop of water was spilt; Nian would sit and strain and strain . . . until the thing hurled itself disastrously across the room. He got heartily fed up with mopping up the mess.

Then came the inevitable day when, completely and utterly by accident, Nian dumped the bowl squarely on Tarq's head like some sort of crazy hat. Tarq was so thoroughly soaked he had to go and change—which was lucky, because Nian and Varn were near bursting. As soon as Tarq had gone they collapsed. They rolled around the floor and laughed until it hurt.

'How could you?' gasped Varn, at last.

'I didn't mean to,' sobbed Nian, wiping his eyes. 'I just can't control the blasted thing. I do try, but I can't.'

Varn took in a deep breath to convince himself he'd stopped laughing.

'Thank goodness Caul's on retreat,' he observed, for now Caul spent whole days alone, dwelling on Wisdom, in preparation for his entry into the Lordship. 'I think I'd have died if I couldn't have had that laugh.'

Nian nodded, rather sadly, for it wasn't very often they had a chance to laugh.

'Though goodness knows it's not funny,' went on Varn, though still good-humouredly. 'You'll probably be soaking *me* next.'

'Sorry,' said Nian. 'I do try, I really do. But it just doesn't work.' He spoke more sadly still, because he was losing hope that he'd ever be strong enough to fly. And if he couldn't learn to fly then he'd most likely be stuck in the House for ever.

The thought of the House without Varn turned his breakfast porridge cold and leaden inside him.

'You're certainly trying,' agreed Varn.

Nian raised a woebegone face to him. 'I shall have to stay here,' he said. 'I'm sure I shall have to. And . . . and sometimes I can hardly *breathe* for hating the Lords, Varn. At least, not the Lords, exactly, not Tarq,

61

anyway, but the House, their Wisdom, everything. When I think of what they could be doing . . . '

'I know,' said Varn, and he was suddenly serious. 'My home: well, it's the best place in all the worlds, and all that, but you can't walk along the street without tripping over beggars. And half of them are crippled or blind . . . Look, Nian, have a go at flying tonight. Don't give up until you've had a real go. I'll show you what to do.'

'Thanks,' said Nian, quite without hope.

'It'll be interesting,' said Varn, thoughtfully. 'Because the way your power explodes out of you, you may be able to carry me over the wall tonight.'

JHT JHT

As far as Nian could make out, flying was a matter of focusing your powers against the natural force that stuck you to the ground.

'It takes a lot of concentration,' Varn told him. 'You have to sort of despise the whole world: that's what it said in the scroll, anyway. Go on, try it.'

Nian tried it, but it was a peculiar thing to try to do. How many times had his father explained that the world spun like a top and that nothing was easier than to push things out of balance? How many times had Grandy, who had the sharpest ears in the world, told him that she could hear the green rocks of the mountains grinding against each other as they moved, just in the same way as she ground the spices for dinner.

'Are you concentrating?' came Varn's voice, rather impatiently. 'Because nothing's happening.'

Nian swallowed the juices that had formed in his mouth at the thought of Grandy's baking and put aside all memories of home and Grandy's stories. He straightened his back and concentrated hard on his own will, on rising from the world in lordship, like the suns. He lowered the screen in his mind and called up all his powers. He despised the earth. The Lords were right: the cities and valleys were low places, full of ignorance and stupidity. The world was full of fools and it was not fit for his feet to—

'*Watch out!*' shrieked Varn, and Nian, distracted, fell. Fortunately he managed to land on his feet, but he still gave his back quite a nasty jar.

'What did you do that for?' he enquired, irritably, for he had a feeling as if he'd left his stomach up in the air, and he disliked it very much.

'Because you were about to smash into the ceiling,' answered Varn. 'You shot up like a rocket. Didn't you know?'

Nian blinked in surprise. Had he?

'I should have realized that might happen,' Varn went on, rather morosely. 'Still, I suppose there's no harm done.'

Nian was still trying to settle his stomach back in place.

'At least I can sort of do it,' he said. 'And I expect everyone has the same trouble at first.'

Varn opened his mouth. But then he only laughed, gently and mockingly.

'Actually, no,' he said. 'No, most people don't have that problem, little Nian.'

'*Don't* call me that!' snapped Nian, still a bit shaken. 'I tried, all right? I couldn't help it. Perhaps,' he went on, more hopefully, 'perhaps, as I'm so useless, the Lords might throw me out of the House. Do you think they might?'

Varn walked round in a circle. When he spoke it was in a slow, patient voice, as though lecturing to an imbecile.

'My dear minute Nian,' he said. 'Listen to me carefully. I am a very, very gifted person. I am so incredibly gifted that I've managed to protect myself from the power of the House, which no one has ever done before. I'm really something special. Do you understand?'

'Well, yes,' muttered Nian, 'I suppose so. But—'

'Never mind *but*,' said Varn, 'just shut up and listen.'

Nian subsided unwillingly.

'As well as all that, I've worked out how to fly,' went on Varn. 'That's an art that's been lost to the Lords for, ooh, about six hundred years. So that's one more absolutely incredible achievement.'

'Wonderful,' agreed Nian, with a yawn of distaste.

'So now,' Varn continued, a little faster, 'after a whole year of practice, I can hover about a foot above the ground for nearly two minutes. And *that* little Nian, is really *fantastic*!'

'Yes,' said Nian, 'but—'

'And then what happens?' went on Varn, rather wildly, now. 'An *infant*, far too young to have any powers *at all*, comes toddling along and proceeds to throw so much power about he almost scalds me to death in the pool, and then, after two minutes' trying, he zooms up into the air as if he's set for the moon! Don't you realize, you *blithering* little idiot, you fool, you complete *moron*, that you've got more power in you than anyone's ever had before, or even dreamed of?'

'Oh,' said Nian, completely taken aback.

'*Do you think they might throw me out,*' echoed Varn, excitedly. 'Don't you realize the Lords are all hoping you're going to be the Truth Sayer? They're going to hold on to you so tight you can hardly breathe!'

Nian had a weak go at taking this in, but gave up almost straight away. It was all too stupid even to think about.

'But *I* can't be powerful,' he pointed out, 'I mean . . . I mean, I can't *do* anything!'

Varn rolled his eyes.

'I know, I know,' he said, with a sigh. 'I can hardly believe it, either, because you're so incredibly stupid with it. But think about it: Tarq's the most powerful of the Lords, all right? And yet when he warms the pool he fades. Have you noticed that?'

'Yes,' said Nian. 'You do, too.'

Varn scowled.

'Of course I do,' he said irritably. 'It takes such a vast amount of power everybody does—everybody except you, that is. *You* can heat the pool up to scalding point without raising a sweat, can't you? You're colossally powerful, Nian!'

Nian stood and felt very distrustful. Surely this must be some twisted sort of joke.

'What's all this Truth Sayer stuff people keep going on about, anyway?' he asked.

'Oh, for crying out loud!' exclaimed Varn. 'Don't you know *anything*?'

'Not about Truth Sayers,' said Nian.

Varn paced to and fro.

'It's a foretelling,' he said grumpily. 'It says that the House of Truth will decline until there is only a handful of Lords left, and they will have forgotten their purpose. And then it says that a pupil will arrive who will . . . who will rediscover the art of flying.' Varn dragged out those last words slowly and reluctantly.

'But that's you!' exclaimed Nian. 'That means *you're* the Truth Sayer! It was *you* who discovered—'

'Do you think I don't know that?' snapped Varn. 'The foretelling goes on to say that then *another* gifted pupil will come, and that he will rebuild the House and make the Lords blessed throughout the land.'

Nian stood, silent, and thinking.

'But that's all wrong,' he said at last. 'At least, it's not me. I'd quite like to tell the Lords a few truths, but I'm not going to save the House. I don't want it saved. I'm going to escape.'

Varn looked at him very straight.

'When?' he asked. 'Tonight? There's no reason why not. You can fly well enough, I should think, providing you don't bang your head on the stars. Or will you wait a week or two so that you can practise?'

Nian felt hope rising inside him. Escape? Tonight? He'd fly over the wall, and then . . .

And then what? He couldn't go home, nor to any of the other valleys. He could go to a city, perhaps. Perhaps Varn's family . . .

The thought of Varn brought him up short. If he escaped tonight then the Lords would strip Varn

67

of his shield, and then Varn would be imprisoned here for ever.

'Varn!'

'Well?'

'I'll wait until you can fly better,' Nian said. 'We'll escape together, as we said we would.'

There was a short pause and then Varn said, stiffly: 'Thanks.'

'There's no point in trying to escape by myself,' said Nian, for he could feel how much Varn's pride was hurt. 'Really. Because I'm going to have to live in a city, and without you I won't have a clue how to do it. When we escape, may I go with you?'

'That sounds a bargain,' said Varn, though he still sounded rather formal. 'But you know it's going to take me months and months to get good enough, don't you?'

Nian hesitated at the thought of all those months, but then he remembered again that he couldn't go home.

'I'll wait,' he said.

5

Jacob wasn't too sure about the sounds that had been coming from the front room just lately. They could have been coming from a primeval swamp; or an elephant's stomach; or a sewage works; or perhaps even something like a lemonade factory.

There were definitely *bubbles*.

Dad didn't like it. He didn't really like any of the *Wherevers*, but some he was more or less resigned to. He was fairly relaxed about the clunking of massed wind-chimes, probably because they reminded him of the crystal shop, and he was fine with any sort of chanting. Jacob was OK with most things, really, and the rock concerts were *fantastic*, though he had to be careful not to air-drum along to the music, because it totally freaked Dad when he did that. Dad just couldn't cope with the idea that Jacob could hear the *Wherevers*. But, hey, if that was a sign of madness, then being insane wasn't so bad.

When Jacob was in a band, which was going to be some time after the family got enough money to buy him a drum kit, which was going to be some time after Dad got a job, which was going to be some time after

Dad got better, which was . . . Anyway, when Jacob was in a band, he was going to record some of those *Wherever* tracks here. On Earth. In this dimension/ world/astral plane/*Wherever*.

You never knew, he might even get to be just a bit cool. Or famous, even.

Yeah.

He could cope with that.

|||| |||| |

Nian lived in the House of Truth all through the rest
of the summer. That was the most difficult part: once
the snows came, the hunger and cold left him little
energy, even for hating.

Varn talked about the city a lot: about haggling,
and robbers, and slave dealers. Nian listened, and
tried not to think of home—of the scent of mother's
bread, or Grandy's stories, or the snow-melt lushness
of the fields. Of Miri and Tan. Lying and cheating
seemed to be a necessary part of living in a city, and
he hated the thought of it.

But he had nowhere else to go.

Nian studied with Tarq every day. This was seldom
dull, because however hard Nian tried, his powers
remained at uncontrollably high pressure. Tarq was
patient, but Nian got tired of apologizing for smashing things to pieces or setting them on fire.

'It will come,' Tarq would say, soothingly, as something else shattered into a puff of dust. And Nian, his
face burning with frustration and effort, would ask
when? but Tarq would only smile and send him off to
the library to cool down.

So Nian spent a lot of time in the library. He did his best to avoid Firn the librarian, who was always in a mild fuss about something or other, and instead he sought out the dustiest, most private corners, where the scrolls seemed not to have been disturbed for centuries. He liked these oldest scrolls because sometimes they had little pictures of birds and plants in the margins, and he took a strange irresistible delight in torturing himself with pictures of things from home.

These oldest scrolls were written in a peculiar script, but Nian soon worked it out. They were full of the things closest to his heart—sowing times, and healing herbs, and the care of livestock—mostly things he was familiar with, though sometimes he came across something new. What would Father think of these new ideas, that were really old ideas? Would he be willing to try them out?

But Nian would never know. Never. That was the fact of it. He'd never talk to Father again. He'd never see the thatched roof of the Hall, never see any of them, Grandy, Mother, Miri, Tan ever again. Never.

Sometimes that knowledge crippled him so completely that he could hardly stop himself from howling.

But still Nian loved to read the farm-lore of the Lords, and he was disappointed when the next scroll in the rack proved to be written in a different, vigorous hand, and to have no pictures at all. He was casting it aside in disgust when his eyes caught the word *escape*.

But in fact the scroll was nothing to do with escaping from the House: it was still about farming, really, but in quite a different way.

We must examine every part of the world, it began. *Nothing must escape us. For when we have the truth, we have understanding; when we have understanding, we have mastery. Thus shall the Lords rule the world in might and glory.*

Tarq continued to try to teach Nian. He would place a simple roof tile in front of his pupil and bid him explore it. Nian would dive into the tile with his mind, travelling through its chaotic powderiness, until he could smell the earth from which it had come, and the plants that had once grown in it, and the strange lizards which had walked on it. Going deeper still, he could even taste the rock from which the clay had been worn, millions upon millions of years ago. So much knowledge there was, so much power, in one small tile.

But when it came to *using* this knowledge, by levitating the thing, or snapping it and putting it back together again in a different shape, then all this smooth power, that Nian had flown upon like an eagle, dried up and crumbled uselessly to dust and failure.

Tarq was puzzled by this, though never angry.

'It is not a lack of power,' he said. 'Do you find yourself distracted, my son?'

Nian shook his head sadly, for what was there to distract him in this pale desert between the walls of the Outer House and the inaccessible garden?

'Look,' said Varn, one evening; and he flew right up to the ceiling and stayed there for a whole minute before sinking slowly down to the ground. 'Pretty good, huh?'

'Tremendous,' agreed Nian, politely.

Varn grinned.

'Another two weeks and I'll be ready,' he said. 'Then we'll be off to the city, Nian. I can hardly wait.'

Nian opened his mouth to say that he hated the thought of the city, but then he saw Varn's joy, and said nothing.

That night Nian lay awake long after Varn was snoring. He gazed at the shadows of the holm-tree, cast by the full moon, and he thought of the worlds turning together. That was a beautiful idea—beautiful in a way in which few of the things in the House were beautiful. It seemed whole, somehow: like his life at home.

Nian gazed at the soft dangling shadows of the catkins and little leaves of the holm-tree. Then, on impulse, he threw aside his cover and got up. The window was high above his head, but what did that matter when he could fly? Nian felt quietly for his clothes, for the nights were still sharp. He had little more control over his powers than he'd ever had—but he should be able to boost himself up so he could grab hold of the windowsill.

He took a deep breath and concentrated as hard as he could on how much he despised the earth. It was difficult to think something so fiercely untrue, but he gritted his teeth and clenched his fists. Nothing happened, and nothing happened . . . and then, with a sudden violent lunge, the window swooped down at him so fast that it was only by a wild grab at the window frame that he prevented himself from shooting right through and down into the blackness of the garden. He paused for a second to re-swallow his heart, and then he wriggled himself round until he was astride the sill.

The scent of the garden alone was enough to enrapture him. He could pick out the coolness of the tiny muret flowers, and, stronger and more assertive, the heady azurels.

I've missed the goldcups, he thought, with a pang, and, almost without thinking, he laid his hand on the trunk of the holm-tree and swung himself down to the ground.

He came down in a bramble patch, and it was only the absolute necessity of being silent that stopped him saying one of the excellently strong words he'd learned from Varn. He detached himself with difficulty from all the little barbs on the briars and stepped cautiously out into the garden.

It was too dark to see much, even with his strong senses fully alert. He was used to the background colour of the Lords' minds, so he hardly noticed them, but he noticed each little rosette of pale shyflowers, and he noticed the hayfinches sleeping in the trees.

There were butterstars, too, and the stiff finchbell spikes were budding. Nian had gone only a few paces when he came upon a stoneberry tree in full, glorious, moonlit bloom. It was so utterly wonderful after months in the House that he could hardly bear it. He sat down on a patch of thin grass and he tried to take it in.

A year had gone, nearly. Nearly a year, wasted between the walls of the House of Truth. He couldn't waste any more of his life. He'd learned some things, but it was not what he should have been learning.

And soon he'd be in the city, and that wasn't what he wanted, either. His life was not going to be *his* life at all: it was going to be wasted.

There was a clump of finchbells growing by his feet, but the flower spikes were still stiff and new and green. He wished he could see them bloom . . .

. . . and as he wished the stiff stems stretched, and arched, and unfurled themselves into flower.

He stared at them in complete amazement. Had *he* done that? But he couldn't have done. His power always had to be forced from him in an uncontrollable rush, and this had been so gentle and so natural that he'd hardly noticed it.

He scrambled to his feet and made his way across the glade to another clump of finchbells. Again he wished, very gently—and again the flower stalks grew and unfolded until their scent gushed out into the still air.

Nian drew in a deep, tremulous breath of pure wonder. Varn had told him he was powerful, but now for the first time he really believed it was true.

He began to walk uphill. It was wonderful to get away from the encircling wall of the House, but it wasn't long before he was out of breath. All this time in the House with no exercise and little food had made his muscles waste away to straw, and that was *wrong*: he was made with arms and legs, and he should use them. That was how it should be.

At the very top of the mountain was a great stone block. It seemed to have been been carved, but it was crusted with lichen and crumbled by the frosts of so many winters that there was no telling what it was meant to be. Nian sat down and regarded it. For a little while it looked like a fat squatting man, and then it looked like a table, and then it looked like a fat pillow . . .

Nian sat himself up hastily. He must go back to the House before he fell asleep. But it was hard to think of going back, when the garden had set his heart vibrating with the spring.

This is my proper place, he thought. Perhaps everyone had their proper place. For Varn it was the city and for Nian it was the country. And for some people, like Tarq, it might even be the House of the Lords of Truth.

I've got to be in my proper place, he thought.

But how?

He sat, following his thoughts round and round as he'd done a thousand times before, even though he knew there was nowhere in the world he could go.

But then Nian felt a faint stirring inside himself, as if he'd caught a glimpse of some faint hope. What had he just thought, that had made his heart jolt within him? *He knew there was nowhere in the world* . . .

That was it.

That was it! There was nowhere in the world—this world. But there might be somewhere in another world. The Tarhun of another world would know nothing about him. Or perhaps another world might have no Tarhun at all. Boys with gifts might be allowed to stay in their homes, there. And they might welcome a boy around who could make plants grow faster. Yes, if he was out of the reach of the Tarhun then he could use his gifts; it would be easy to be wanted, then.

And this was the place where the worlds touched. Varn had said so. And Nian had strong powers. But did he have powers enough to take that one small forbidden step to another world?

Well, he had two weeks to find out.

Nian glanced round hastily, as if someone might have read his thoughts; there was no one, but a haze of dangerous orange had appeared above the black line of the House. Nian mustn't be discovered here.

He made his way back to the holm-tree. He was tired, and it took a series of great efforts to haul himself up to the window, and when he got there it seemed easier to drop down than to try to fly. Varn snorted a little as Nian's feet hit the floor, but he didn't wake. Nian threw off his clothes, burrowed his way under his cover, and fell instantly into a deep and dreamless sleep.

$\cancel{||||}\ \cancel{||||}\ ||$

The next few days were unlike any others Nian had known in the House, for he was both furiously busy and desperately frightened at what he was hoping to do. He snatched at every chance to search the library for mentions of other worlds. He did find something that said that if anyone crossed from one world to another then both worlds would tremble, and crack, and finally explode into a mist of swirling motes, but that was in a scroll which was otherwise full of fussy, irritating methods of doing fussy, irritating things, like buttoning your coat by Wisdom. Anyway, it couldn't be true, because according to the tales a whole army had already invaded this world: and here they all were, still, after all.

Another scroll failed to mention the end of the worlds, but contented itself with a warning of visions of people with odd haircuts.

Nian read everything he could find. One scroll was full of sums. He couldn't begin to understand them, but the conclusion was clear enough. *So it can be seen*, it said at the end, rather smugly, *that a passageway to one particular world will be open only for a few days; after that, it will disappear for many generations.*

That threw Nian off balance again. He'd pretty much decided on trying to escape to a new world, but he wasn't nearly so sure about never being able to come back again. He spent one whole night just lying on his mat and thinking about home. In the end he comforted himself with the thought that he wasn't very likely to succeed.

Nian made his first attempt to open a passageway to a new world a week before Varn was planning to go over the wall. Nian was lucky that the Lords only went into the garden once or twice a year, as a sort of festival; though the Lords' idea of a festival consisted of missing a meal and perhaps smiling once.

Nian hadn't told Varn about his change of plan. He didn't have the energy to waste time arguing, especially as he might well have to go with Varn in any case.

The night was cold and cloudy and damp and not in the least inspiring.

Nian started his experiments with a twig. He took it up to the statue, which was as far away from the House as he could get. He sat down, placed the twig carefully in front of him, straightened his back in the attitude of Wisdom, and wondered what on earth to do.

He spent several minutes convincing himself that the other worlds really existed, and several more convincing himself that he was powerful enough to make something happen. This was particularly hard because his power, that had been so strong and glorious during his first visit to the garden, had gone and tied itself up in knots again.

In the end he decided there was no harm in trying.

He focused his thoughts on the little twig, trying to push it away with his mind. Nothing happened for several straining seconds . . .

. . . until the twig shot off at a million paces an hour, crashed into the statue, and broke.

Nian said one of the words Varn had taught him.

Then he tried again.

Nian struggled with that twig for over two hours. By that time it was as long as a match stick and Nian was so disgusted that he threw it on the ground and stamped on it. Then he walked round in circles for a few minutes, thinking furiously. Then he had to grin at himself, acknowledge he was tired out, and go back to the House to sleep.

So that was a complete failure.

The next night he fell asleep by accident and didn't wake up till morning, but the night after that he pulled a handful of grass and took that up to the statue. He'd been thinking a lot, and he'd decided to try approaching the problem according to the rules of Truth that Tarq had taught him. He let his mind dive down through the long leaves of the grass, along every vein and into every green cell. He skated along each sharp edge of every leaf, and then back to the root, to the earth. And then he wished them out of the world in the most passionately heartfelt way.

The result—a small but intense bonfire—was discouraging.

So he imagined the worlds spinning in beauty and harmony. He imagined them golden and translucent and shining. He imagined them turning together, touching, but separate.

Yes, he thought, appreciatively: this is how it is.

Then he imagined himself inside one of the lovely spheres. He reached up and grasped the material of the thing and tore a hole in it so he could get out.

But straight away he knew that was wrong. The whole picture turned cardboard and unreal in his mind.

Perhaps the Lords were right to try to stop travel between the worlds.

Disheartened, Nian went back to his sleeping mat.

The next night, Nian, who had been thinking harder than he'd ever thought in his life, tried something new. Instead of making holes in the worlds, which hurt them, he'd build bridges, instead.

But it was hard to imagine a bridge that was right for the glistening spheres. He tried humped stone bridges and wavering rope bridges, arches of alabaster and spans of wood, but he could tell as soon as he called them to mind that they were just *wrong*.

Nian was working with a pebble that night. He sat cross-legged and glared at it for a long time, and it sat there as if it didn't care. It was an ugly pebble, Nian decided, not fit to be transported to another world. He'd smash it—fry it with a spurt of Wisdom.

He caught hold of it to hurl it away, but even as his fingers closed on it they felt the roughness of its surface and he had to pause to look. The pebble was crazed with tiny cracks—just like nearly every other one Nian had ever seen. But still . . .

I couldn't make one, thought Nian, turning it over in his hand. He couldn't even model one from clay. It was ugly, but it was beyond anything he could even dream of, and his powers were stronger than anyone's had ever been.

Nian sat with the pebble in his hands and again he called to mind the vision of the golden translucent spheres. He watched them turning for a while, and he realized that the picture was complete in itself. Whatever he added would be wrong.

The mountains move, Grandy used to say. *Sometimes I can hear them, creaking and grating. Once, long ago, there was a mother world, but the rocks in its belly stirred and cracked open and sent out a fountain of stones that went up and up, large and small, and now they hang for ever in the skies.*

But where *are* all those other worlds? thought Nian. How far away? What is it like to be so far from everything I have ever known?

He looked up, and saw the stars, multitudes of them, shining.

Shining.

Suddenly, without thinking, he held the pebble up in his hand as though offering it to someone.

And it vanished.

6

Nan gave a long suspicious sniff as Jacob sat down next to her at the dining table.

'Susan! Susan! What's the boy been up to?' she demanded. 'He smells peculiar!'

Jacob made a face. He'd been miming along to Keith Moon, which was bound to make you a bit sweaty, but not that much more than usual, he'd have thought.

Robyn sniffed too, and a puzzled look crossed her face.

'It's like perfume,' she said. 'A really old-fashioned flowery one. Or . . . I'll tell you what it's like. It's like an air-freshener: *mountain-fresh*.'

'Can't abide those things,' said Nan, fretfully. 'One stink upon another, that's all they are.'

Robyn gave Jacob an odd look.

'Jake,' she said, 'what have you been doing?'

'Nothing,' said Jacob, uneasily. 'My technology project.'

Technology was a magic word in Jacob's family. It worked sort of like hypnosis. Once you said it, people's faces glazed over and they started talking about something else.

Jacob scooped up a forkful of mushy peas. The really great thing about them being so hard up is that they got to eat fantastic food.

He was surprised that the others could smell the flowers, though. Nan had been out all afternoon taking Mrs Hinde to the WI, so he'd been working on his technology project (a snare drum) in the front room. It had been quiet in there, for once, except for the occasional hooting of owls, and the sighing of the wind. Peaceful. But, oddly, it had *smelt of flowers*.

Jacob had never known *smells* come through from the *Wherevers* before and he had certainly never known anyone else but Dad pick up on anything *Wherever*ish. He was afraid this meant that something new had happened. The noises weren't too much of a problem, except that they made Dad jumpy, but *smells* might be a pain. They certainly would be if Nan could pick them up: Nan was really fierce about her front room. It was lucky Jacob had noticed that pebble on the carpet in there, and kicked it away out of sight into the fireplace, or Nan would have been nagging away about it for days.

But still, no one was suffering yet, so there was no point in worrying.

All the same, this time it took Jacob until halfway through his shepherd's pie to banish the problem of the *Wherevers* from his mind.

$$\text{卌 卌|||}$$

Sending the pebble into a different world was a tremendous achievement, but still it upset Nian a great deal. The pebble was gone, goodness knew where, down some passageway that he had opened up, and *there was no getting it back*. That was the thing. Yes, Nian wanted to live in the countryside, and to be a farmer, but what he really wanted was his family and his home.

There would be no coming back.

He'd be no worse off, of course. But his insides still hurt. And he dreamed about them all.

He found himself filled with bitterness; he began to hate the Lords with a new fervour, even the harmless ones like Firn and Tarq.

Once we have found the truth, then we have the mastery: that was the principle they all worked to. But Nian could find the truth all right. When he dived with his mind into a tile, or a stone, or a leaf, he was sure he went further, deeper, than any of the Lords. Even Varn did little more than dabble on the surface, compared with him.

So it wasn't the truth that brought mastery, but . . .

If something went wrong, and Nian was caught trying to escape, then Tarq (or all the Lords together, most likely) would strip away Nian's protection, and then the power of the House would conquer him, destroy him.

But—and this was it, this was it—*but they wouldn't use the truth to do it.* They would use knowledge, yes, even understanding, but only to defeat what they found. They would call up an opposite of the truth, an anti-truth, to defeat him.

That was what the Lords did.

Yes.

Their Wisdom, their power, was not truth at all, for there was no power in that.

This was the House of Lies.

During the next couple of nights Nian sent several more pebbles out of the world. He also sent a bunch of finchbells, and, as an experiment, a large blue beetle. The beetle vanished as easily as everything else had done, and showed no signs of exploding, or dying, or feeling any pangs of agony. Nian hoped that was a sign that the vanishing process wasn't painful. Or, indeed, fatal.

Being in the House wasn't much more than a living death, anyway, so he had little to lose, whatever happened.

This was a good argument, though strangely unconvincing.

That evening Varn made an announcement.

'I'm ready to go,' he said, as they washed up. 'Tonight I'm going to rest, and tomorrow I'm going to fast so my powers are strong. So we're leaving tomorrow night.'

Nian drew in a deep breath. But he said nothing.

‖‖ ‖‖ ||||

Nian lay on his mat and stared up through the darkness. One more day.

Varn would be better off without him, of course. But Nian would have to explain. Perhaps Varn could take a message to Nian's family—or send one. Yes, tomorrow Nian would write a letter, and when it arrived the animal doctor would be able to read it out to them. And then they'll know not to expect him. Ever.

Nian's mind was too busy for sleep. He got up, boosted himself up to the windowsill, and climbed down to the garden.

The garden was familiar, now, but still entrancingly beautiful. The finchbells were in full bloom, though there were two clumps close to his path that were withered and finished. Nian passed by them with averted eyes and an inescapable feeling of guilt.

Gradually the peace of the garden overtook him. This was a lovely place, but there was a new world just a day away. What would it be like? Might there be mermaids or dragons? Snow, or sunshine? Perhaps he might go to the sea, that he had only ever seen as a shadow or a glitter far away beyond the mountains.

He was so busy wondering if poisonous insects in every world wore warning stripes of black and yellow that he didn't notice anything different about the statue.

He didn't notice anything until something on top of it moved.

Nian stopped as suddenly as if he'd walked into a wall.

A man. There was a man there. And it must be one of the Lords.

Run?

No, freeze. He can't have seen you yet. Who is it? Firn has poor sight.

Find out.

Nian sent a spurt of Wisdom at the figure sitting on the statue. Firn or Rago or . . . but no. No. Its leggings were too baggy round the calves, and its tunic was too short in the arms. And it was much, much too young—only a boy—and its hair glinted orange, not grey or white.

The figure snatched round its head and pointed it at Nian as he stood frozen in dismay.

And then it spoke. '*Hooz thair?*' it said.

And it spoke in no language Nian had ever heard of.

'Who are you?' Nian asked fiercely. 'How did you get here?'

But the figure only sighed, and scratched its orange head.

'*Grayt,*' it said, as if to itself. '*Thatz orl ei need!*'

This boy certainly wasn't a Lord—nor one of the Tarhun, either—a stranger, then: which was impossible. Nian stared at him, appalled and fascinated. He'd never seen hair that colour in his life.

'*Doo yoo speek inglish?*' said the orange-haired boy, rather loudly, but without much hope. '*par lay voo frarn say? Sprecken zee doich?*'

These were questions, but that was all Nian could tell. What was this boy doing here? And what did he want? And, most vitally, how could Nian get rid of him before the Lords discovered them?

'Go back home!' said Nian, as intensely as he could. 'This is—this is a holy garden, and only the Lords of Truth are allowed here!'

The strange boy spread out his hands in a sorry-but-I-can't-help-you gesture.

'*Karnt undastand,*' he said. '*No comprarnday. Inglish. Er . . . frend. Mee neiss gei, yes? Oooooooo nikkerz, how kan ei get throo?*'

Nian gazed at him, distrustful and puzzled. This boy must be hugely powerful to have got past the power-net and then through the Inner House. But despite that he didn't seem to have any purpose. In fact he seemed lost, bewildered—and he didn't even speak the right language.

The stranger sighed again and settled himself more comfortably on the statue.

'*Mee Jaycub,*' he said, pointing to his chest with one finger. '*Jaycub.*'

There was no mistaking that gesture. Nian did it himself.

'Nian,' he said.

'*Well, thatz sumthing*,' went the stranger, incomprehensibly. '*Wot next? Tayk mee too yor leeda? Ei karnt eevn arsk wair ei am! Now, doo ei trei too teech this gei inglish, or wot?*'

This is hopeless, thought Nian. He made the effort to sense the boy's—Jaycub's—mind, and he found it mostly surprised, but with a little edging of amusement and curiosity.

'*Just leik a film*,' went on Jaycub. '*Enni minnit now an innormus grate terradaktill ull kum owt ov the skei. Thoh if thiss woz a film, yood speek inglish.*'

Perhaps Nian had better go and wake up Varn so they could escape straight away. But however had this *idiot* got here—and why couldn't he have waited another couple of days?

The boy Jaycub pointed to the thing he was sitting on.

'*Stohn*,' he said, clearly and loudly.

The clearness and loudness made it clear that this was a piece of instruction.

'*Stohn*,' repeated Nian, but then the ridiculousness of the situation struck him so forcibly that he laughed. The garden rang oddly with the echo of that laugh, but Jaycub was grinning back at him.

'*Eim beeginning to undastand how robinsun kroosoh must hav felt*,' he said, and Nian could hear that this was a joke. Perhaps there was some way to understand Jaycub's words. Perhaps, if Nian tried, he could find a way into Jaycub's mind.

'Talk,' Nian said, encouragingly.

'Talk?' Jaycub repeated the word, but he was obviously puzzled by it.

'Yes.' Nian nodded, pointed at his mouth, and then made waving motions to indicate speech rolling out. Jaycub shrugged, but he began to speak. Nian listened, concentrating as hard as he could, trying to catch the meaning of the mind behind the odd jerky sounds.

'*Well, itz a chaynj too hav sumwun wonting mee too yooz mei mowth*,' Jaycub began, and Nian held his breath so he could focus his Wisdom as strongly as he could. '*Yoozyurlee itz shut up, Jayk, or you can't still* be hungry all the time.'

Nian listened, hardly able to believe it, as the sounds shifted, coloured, and resolved themselves into a clear meaning.

'Now you should hear my grisly old nan,' Jacob went on, conversationally. '"I'm sure that boy's got worms, Susan," she goes, and, I mean, it's not even as if she has to pay for my food, is it?'

Nian wasn't sure whether he was more amazed at being able to understand, or at what Jacob was saying. He'd been expecting something about the fact that they were in just about the most dangerous place in the world, not some drivel about Jacob's grandmother.

Nian needed the answers to a lot of questions. Well, if he could understand, he could speak—if he could get his tongue round the sounds.

'Shut up,' he said, politely. The sh sound was difficult, and it seemed strange to end a word with a p, but he made quite a good attempt at it.

Jacob jumped.

'So you *can* speak English!' he exclaimed.

Nian had to think for quite a long time to assemble enough words to reply.

'I can speak English now,' he said. 'No comprendez a minute. Can now.'

Jacob's eyes widened.

'Wow!' he said. 'This is like *Dungeons and Dragons* or something. Or *The Hitch-hikers' Guide*. What a *dream*! Except . . . you know, I didn't know I had the imagination to make up anything as solid as this. What are you, an android, or a super-intelligent pan-dimensional being?'

Nian shook his head, partly to signify *no,* and partly to settle the mind-blowing idea of *android. Pan-dimensional* came over only as a vague blur, but this seemed to be because Jacob hadn't got much idea what it meant himself.

'I suppose this *is* a dream?' went on Jacob, frowning. 'Because it's funny, but I can't actually remember going to sleep. I mean, the last thing I really *remember* is clearing up all those pebbles and bits of grass and disgusting rotten bluebells that someone—I suppose it must have been Dad, really, he's got a memory like a sieve—dumped in Nan's front room. And then . . . yes . . . I saw this enormous great beetle coming across the carpet from the fireplace—big as a cockroach, I'm not joking—and it was *bright electric blue*. So I went to corner it, but the carpet sort of melted into stuff like toffee, only hairier . . . and by the time I'd finished freaking out I was here. So I suppose a dream's the best option, really,' he went on, reflectively. 'It's either that or I've somehow managed to fall into a *Wherever*, or I've gone completely bonkers. Mind you, between Robyn and Nan, anyone'd lose their grip on reality.'

Nian was too struck with awe and horror to answer. This boy was from another world—*the* other world— the world Nian was planning to escape to. All the things Nian had sent out of the world had ended up in Jacob's grandmother's front room, and the passage-way Nian had made had somehow sucked Jacob back through to the garden.

It works, he thought, his heart beating fast. It really works!

So that meant there was nothing to stop him.

There was nothing to stop him going to a completely different world.

$$\text{卌 卌 卌}$$

Jacob looked all round. He was tall, but as ungainly as a three-legged marsh-ox.

'Just the one moon, I see,' he remarked. 'And a standard oxygen-nitrogen atmosphere. Well, that's a relief.'

'No comprendez,' said Nian, his wits still scattered. Jacob grinned.

'Neither do I, really,' he admitted. 'It's just what people say on Sci-Fi programmes. Hey, or is this a pre-industrial society?'

There were so many words in this that failed to make sense that Nian began to wonder if the shock had made him lose the ability to understand Jacob's language.

'No comprendez,' he said again.

'Oh well, never mind,' said Jacob, 'it doesn't matter. What shall we do? I suppose I'd better not stay long, or I'll be getting into trouble—into even *more* trouble, that is. Nan's convinced I messed up her precious front room, and she's practically been calling for the re-introduction of the death-penalty. Silly woman. Not that I think all this is actually real, obviously. At least, not *really* real.'

Nian nodded eagerly.

'You can't stay long,' he said, getting hopelessly tangled trying to say the *ong* sound. 'Or I'll be getting into trouble with my grisly—' he broke off, not knowing the word.

'Parents?' suggested Jacob. 'Teacher?'

'No—yes,' said Nian. 'Teacher.'

'So this is a school, then. Honestly, I manage to stagger nearly to Friday, and then when I get sucked into another world I go and end up in a school. Mind you, I suppose it's better than having bears and wolves and wild beasts all over the place. Or pterodactyls, as I said. Or being at the bottom of a lake with all the leeches and fish. So . . . this must be a boarding school, I suppose, as it's the middle of the night. Unless you're all nocturnal, of course; though you don't look as if you've got huge bug-eyes, from what I can see of you. Hey, you aren't *green*, are you?'

'Boarding school,' said Nian. 'Grisly. Grisly. Disgusting. No going home.'

Jacob blinked at Nian through the darkness, genuinely shocked.

'What, never?'

'Never. Never.'

In the darkness Nian could feel Jacob considering this.

'Not even when you grow up? Hey, this isn't—it's not a loony bin, is it?'

Nian had to laugh again, though it was frustrating to know so few words. He could understand everything Jacob said, and he could repeat it, but he lacked lots of essential words, like *danger* and *wisdom*.

'Well, I might as well have a look round,' said Jacob, consideringly, 'because, as I said, I'll have to be going home fairly soon. Though what you should *really* be doing is inviting me to sit down to lashings of ginger beer and seedy cake. Either that, or trying to kill me because you think I'm the devil. Or a god. That'd be quite cool, actually. I should have brought my ghetto-blaster with me for special god-like effects: some mega-watt bass. John Bonham, or Roger Taylor, or someone.'

The very last thing Nian wanted was Jacob nosing around the House.

'School disgusting,' he said fiercely. 'Think you devil.'

But Jacob showed no signs of alarm.

'Hey, come on, there's no need to be so twitchy,' he said. 'I mean, it's the middle of the night, and there's no one here. Anyway, I'm probably destined to sort out your evil wizard or war-troll or whatever it is that's bothering you. It's always your stranger from another world that fixes that sort of thing. Don't worry, I won't be demanding a reward—apart from the throne, absolute power, and the undying affection of all the people. I suppose you don't have a tradition of welcoming strangers with displays of naked female belly-dancing, do you?'

He spoke in light, flippant tones and Nian felt a strong urge to take him by the throat and shake him, because getting Jacob to go home was absolutely, desperately important.

But at least Jacob had given him some useful words. Nian gathered all his powers to use them.

'You're in a world,' he said. 'Comprendez? Not your world. You go home now, I come to your world. Not now . . . not now, but night coming.'

Jacob gawped at him.

'*You* come to *my* world?' he repeated, taken aback. 'Hey, yeah, but . . . what do you want to do that for?'

'Here danger. Grisly, disgusting. No home. I come to your world and have home.'

Jacob failed to look honoured, pleased, or even welcoming.

'You have home?' he echoed. 'But . . . hey, come off it! You can't just expect people to provide you with housing. Have you been watching too many soaps, or what?'

Nian's heart sank. Jacob's words conjured up a vision of a crowded, regulated world: a world that was all city. But it couldn't really be like that. After all, the people must eat (mustn't they?). And if they ate, there must be farming of some sort. Mustn't there?

He looked doubtfully at the other boy.

'I come, I can provide me,' he said.

Jacob heaved a sigh.

'No you can't, you're no older than me. And you can't even speak English. I mean, I'll do what I *can*,' he went on, 'I mean, of course I will. But I won't be able to feed you and look after you for all that long. There's hardly room for us in the house as it is. Where will you live?'

'On a—' Nian stopped short, lacking the word, not even knowing if Jacob's language had a word for *farm*.

'This world grisly,' he said, 'I can't live here. Danger. You go home now, or there's danger. I come, night coming.'

Jacob shrugged.

'Oh well, I suppose you know best,' he said. 'Though it seems a bit of a waste to go home so soon: all I've done is sit in the dark and talk to someone who can't speak English.' He got up, and stumbled rather. 'Wow, your gravity's really low,' he commented. 'That's a real waste: I bet you don't even play cricket.'

A wonderful image came into Nian's mind with the word *cricket*: a vision of a lush green field spotted with white-clad figures who were all intent on . . . on something he couldn't quite catch hold of. His impression, on the whole, was that it was a religious ceremony. He'd opened his mouth to frame a question when something squirmed on the edge of his mind: a flare of acid green.

He forgot all about cricket, then. The colour was beginning to spread. That meant something—someone—was out here in the garden with them, and getting nearer. Getting nearer fast.

Nian seized Jacob's arm.

'Sh!' he hissed. Jacob jumped at his touch, and looked round, but not in the right direction.

'What is it?' he asked.

The colour was so strong now it was almost too bright to look at. It wasn't Varn: it was too bright for Varn.

'Come!' breathed Nian, and pulled Jacob into the shade of a tassel tree. The blob of colour was moving outwards, now, and separating into different shapes. There must be several people in the garden: all of the Lords, perhaps.

Nian had to get right away, out of the garden at once before he was discovered. And Jacob must come with him, for there was no time to explain.

It was easy for Nian to move quickly and quietly because he could sense obstacles even when he couldn't see them, but Jacob crashed about like a herd of stampeding hornbuck. And every time he walked into a branch, or stubbed his toe, he swore.

'It's no good *shushing*,' Jacob muttered. 'I nearly fractured my skull just then. And it *hurts*.'

'*Danger,*' breathed Nian, and pulled him on.

The Lords seemed to be making their way towards the statue. Why did there have to be a festival on this night of all nights!

'I hope my nan gets pulled here too,' said Jacob, with his face in a patch of mud. 'The old bat'd soon sort all this lot out.'

Nian went cold with horror at the thought. The Lords were a dopey bunch, but even they could hardly miss a full-sized old lady if she popped up amongst them. And what if one of the Lords suddenly found himself in Jacob's nan's front room? This was all desperately awful. Nian waited, breathing quietly, as the slow footsteps of a Lord—Rago, it was—passed by them. Then Nian tugged Jacob up.

101

'Come!' he whispered, and led Jacob through the tangle of the garden to the holm-tree. Jacob climbed it easily, his long arms and legs giving him an efficient, ladder-climbing look. He was waiting by the window when Nian pulled himself up.

'In here?' Jacob asked. 'Do we jump down? How far is it? Haven't you got a light, or a lamp or something? I can't see anything.'

For Jacob, it was a drop into pitch darkness.

'I jump now,' said Nian. 'You jump soon.'

He dropped lightly down into the sleeping room and listened for the deep breathing that meant Varn and Caul were still asleep. Jacob was uncomfortably straddling the windowsill with most of his body outside.

'I'll hang by my hands from the window sill,' Jacob said, 'and then you can guide my feet down, OK?'

'OK.'

Jacob wriggled round and lowered himself to the length of his arms. Nian got hold of his thick legs. Jacob's feet were less than eight spans off the floor.

'Not far,' whispered Nian. 'Your skull more far. Now: *jump*.'

Jacob let go. He fell neatly, almost as lightly as Nian.

A second after Jacob's large feet touched the floor Nian remembered that Jacob couldn't fly.

Which meant that now Jacob was trapped in the House.

|||| |||| ||||

Nian was so appalled at the complete and utter stupidity of what he'd done that he could hardly believe it. But there was no time even to mutter Varn's gory words. Nian had to get Jacob away, out of the room, and then . . . he hadn't a clue what then.

Jacob flinched at the unexpected touch of Nian's hand in the darkness, but Nian didn't dare risk a reassuring word. He steered Jacob between Varn's and Caul's sleeping bodies, and out along the black corridor to the schoolroom.

'This is school,' Nian whispered. 'You stay here. No danger here.'

Jacob put an uncertain hand against the wall. He seemed suddenly very out of breath, and the sound of him panting was magnified by the empty room. And then, before Nian could do anything about it, Jacob was sliding down the cold stone wall into a sitting position.

'What's the matter?' asked Nian, forgetting to speak Jacob's language.

Jacob put his hands on the ground to support himself.

'The air's gone thick,' he gasped. 'It's too . . . too hard to breathe. I *can't breathe in here*, Nian!'

The air? Nian gazed round through the darkness. He seldom gave them a thought, but of course the mists of power were shifting all round them, heavy and curdled as old cream.

Jacob's breathing had a rough edge, now, and his head was hanging down nearly to his knees. He was on the verge of passing out. Nian, in a panic, tried to scoop the mists away with his hands, but it was like paddling water: the mists parted, but they slid together again. They were finding their way into Jacob's lungs and suffocating him.

Nian half got up to run for help, for Varn—for Tarq, even—but Jacob's breathing was getting slower and there wasn't time.

Nian knelt down beside Jacob again and grabbed at the warm fleeces round Jacob's face, but still the stuff slipped through his grasp, under and round and through and away, as slippery as eels.

And now Jacob's head was crashing with a horrible thud the last few inches onto the stone flags of the floor. Nian caught up his hand, tugged at it, just to make him move, seem more alive.

But Jacob's hand felt so horribly smooth and some-how oily that he dropped it at once. Jacob was from a different world, of course, (was Jacob a *boy*, at all?) but even so his hand felt . . . there was no life in it. It felt dead, decaying.

Jacob was hardly breathing, but he was no ghost,

Nian was sure of it. Not yet, he wasn't. Nian couldn't make the mists go away, but perhaps he could shield Jacob, just as he was shielded himself. He was going to have to try; he was going to have to succeed, too.

Nian called up his powers. He concentrated on the invisible membrane that covered him all over, but which he hardly ever thought about, now. He imagined it peeling loose from his skin and expanding outwards and outwards until it made a bubble-like sphere round his body. Yes, that was right. He waited until the thing was six feet round, and then he stepped astride Jacob's body. The thin sphere stretched down over Jacob, clinging to every inch of tunic and leggings and hair and skin; then, very carefully, Nian split it open along Jacob's back, slipped it invisibly down over him and under him, and closed it up again in seamless perfection.

Jacob gave a long whooping gasp, and then another, and then another, while Nian stood over him, dizzy with effort and relief.

Jacob was panting out swear words, now. They didn't make much sense, but Nian could feel the strength of feeling behind them.

'I nearly died just then,' gasped Jacob, after a while. 'What the *hell* happened?'

'Air thick,' said Nian, with few words to explain. 'Not thick now.'

Jacob pushed himself up to a sitting position, and Nian stepped to one side to make room for him. The invisible membrane that enclosed them was stretchy, and there was easily room for them both.

'Oh damn, oh damn, oh damn,' said Jacob, still panting. 'It's not going to go thick again, is it?'

'No. No, not now.'

'Well, thank God for that,' he said, rather shakily. 'Good grief. Look, Nian, what's going on? I know there were people outside, but they weren't exactly rampaging about shouting *exterminate*, were they? I mean, it's difficult to imagine they're more dangerous than being in a place with no air.'

Nian looked at Jacob, who wasn't quite looking at him because they were in pitch darkness, and felt exasperated and frustrated.

'I speak grisly English,' he said. 'I can't . . . I can't speak this danger.'

Jacob sighed.

'Oh . . . oh, hell's bells. All right. You can understand and answer, though, can't you. OK. Who *are* those people? Are they really cruel to you?'

Nian had to say *no* to that, because the Lords hadn't beaten him or taunted him, and they'd healed him when he was hurt.

'But you have to stay in this place for ever?'

'Yes,' said Nian. 'For ever.'

'But you say it's not a mental hospital,' went on Jacob, thoughtfully. 'Hey, you don't all have some horrible disease, do you? Leprosy, or something? Or . . . is this a prison?'

Nian shook his head.

'But who else stays locked up for ever? Lunatics, lepers, criminals . . . hang on, you're not *monks*?'

That was a strange word that meant many things, but it fitted the Lords in some ways. So Nian said *yes*, but with something in his tone to show he had reservations about it. Jacob was silent for a few seconds.

'That's just terrible,' he said, at last, soberly. 'No one should be forced into something like that. Don't you *ever* get out? Not even to go to the shops, or for walks or anything? Or for holidays?'

Nian thought about the Lords shopping, and laughed mirthlessly. It served as an answer. Jacob nodded, as if his mind was made up.

'All right,' he said. 'In that case I'll do what I can to help. How many boys are there in here?'

That was complicated: too complicated to explain it at all properly. When Jacob heard about Varn, he insisted that he must be given his own chance to come to his world, too. Nian did try to argue, but things had got so far out of control that he was quite relieved to have an excuse to fetch Varn.

Nian took the time to separate the power-membrane very carefully into two separate bubbles, one for each of them, and then he slipped back to the sleeping room to wake Varn from his deep, delicious, and necessary slumbers. Explaining about Jacob wasn't easy. Varn was first incredulous, and then indignant, and then completely furious.

'I'm really sorry,' whispered Nian, humbly, all the while in terror of Caul waking up, or the Lords coming back in from the garden, or Jacob deciding to go off by himself. 'But now he's trapped in the House and I don't know what to do.'

Nian was almost blinded by the white-hot dazzle of Varn's rage and fear.

'You little *idiot*! You *fool*! You *cretin*!' Varn said, in the smallest, most intense whisper. 'What the *blazes* have you been up to? No, don't tell me,' he said. 'Just let's get rid of him before he causes any more trouble.'

Varn counted the doorways with his fingertips as he hastened along towards the schoolroom. 'What's this creature like?' he muttered, sourly. 'How many heads has he got?'

Nian was surprised first at the question, and then at the answer.

'He's just ordinary, except that his hair's orange. He talks a funny language—but I can understand it, mostly.'

'Does he have powers?'

'No. I don't think he knows anything about them. But he says . . . '

Varn swung round suspiciously and Nian walked into him.

'He says what?' Varn demanded.

Nian gulped, and said, 'He says that he'll help us start up a new life in his world, if we like.'

Varn seized the material at Nian's throat and lifted him nearly off the ground.

'Why you little . . . ' growled Varn. Then he snorted and pushed him away. 'So all this time I've been helping you, you've been planning to go off without me.'

Nian, ashamed, and with no answer, pushed open the door to the schoolroom.

The night was drawing to an end, and Nian got his first glimpse of Jacob using his eyes and not his powers. Jacob's silhouette was longer even than Varn's, though he had an awkwardness that suggested he was growing fast. Jacob peered tensely through the darkness, but still there was something about him that spoke of a lifetime of ease and security.

'This is Varn,' said Nian, in English. 'He is . . . he think you are here disgusting.'

'Yeah,' said Jacob. 'But then, being sucked here and then three-quarters suffocated hasn't been the most relaxing experience, either. Does he want to come to live in my world?'

Varn's answer, when Nian had explained, was brisk, terse, and untranslatable.

'You're mad,' Varn said angrily. 'You don't even know where you're going. You'll end up sold as a slave, or dying in a gutter.'

'But perhaps I won't have to live in a city, there,' said Nian. 'I'm sorry, Varn. I truly am. But living in a city would nearly kill me.'

Varn glared at Nian; and then shook his head.

'You realize that once the worlds move on you won't be able to come home, don't you.'

'Of course I do.'

'Then you're an even bigger idiot than I thought. I mean, who *is* this boy? He may look stupid, but he must be incredibly powerful to have got here. Why do you trust him when you don't trust . . . ' Varn came to an abrupt halt. Then he finished, unconvincingly, 'anyone else.'

'*Ei tayk it thee arnserz noh,*' said Jacob. It took Nian a little while to work out what he meant, because his mind was wincing away from the realization of how much he'd hurt Varn.

'Please come too,' he said to Varn. 'I want us to go together. I need you to help me.'

'Well I won't!' snapped Varn. 'And neither should you. *This* is your world, Nian.'

'But there's no *place* for me here!' burst out Nian. 'I need to be somewhere where I can live in the countryside and make things grow—and use my powers if I want to—without worrying about the Tarhun!'

'But it'll be fine in the city,' said Varn. 'I know it will.'

'*Eid reellee betta bee gohing hohm soon beefor eim missed,*' said Jacob.

But that was just one more problem.

'He needs to go home,' Nian told Varn, despairingly, 'but I think he has to go back from the statue in the garden, and I don't know how to get him there. He can't fly up to the window, and . . . and all the Lords are out in the garden.'

Varn swore again.

'So now I know why you woke me up,' he muttered. 'Because you need help. I'd let you stew in it, if it wasn't going to mess up my own escape.'

'*Which wayz owt?*' asked Jacob. '*Eil get intoo trubbl if eim too long and then mei pairents mite not let yoo stay.*'

'He's got to go home,' said Nian. 'Whatever are we going to do?'

Varn let out another long multi-coloured stream of steaming words. Then he stopped, and took a deep breath.

'All right,' he said. 'Well, there is one good thing: if the Lords are in the garden, then they must have gone out through a door. So we just have to find it, that's all. Come on.'

He turned and plunged back into the corridor. Nian beckoned to Jacob and then, remembering he couldn't see well, caught hold of his shirt and pulled him out of the room. 'Way out,' he whispered.

Varn strode ahead of them, guiding them along the endless curved inside wall of the House. This part of the House was new to Nian, but it was like the rest, pale and empty. Occasionally there was a small window set up high, like the one in the sleeping room.

The dawn was well advanced, now, and once Jacob could see he, easily the strongest and fittest, took the lead. That was why it was Jacob who found the doorway to the garden.

It was also Jacob who came face to face with Tarq.

||||| ||||| |||||||

Nian, a little way behind, heard Jacob's gasp. Then to his horror he heard Tarq's voice, high with wonder.

'Welcome to the House of Truth,' Tarq said.

Nian stopped dead. This was the end of everything. The end of his hopes, of his escape, of his life. But Varn had grabbed his sleeve and was dragging him on.

'No!' hissed Nian, frantically trying to wrench himself free. 'Tarq's there!'

'I know! Quick, or we'll be too late!'

A little way ahead a doorway was casting a hazy oblong of pinkish light across the floor. It was almost full day, now: light enough for Tarq to see them clearly even without using his powers.

'Lord!' gasped Varn, out of breath with hurrying. 'We felt your distress, so we came as fast as we could. What has happened?'

Tarq took his eyes from Jacob for a moment.

'I am not distressed,' he said mildly, 'only very greatly astonished to find a stranger here.'

'A stranger?' echoed Varn. He stared left and right and all round the room. 'Truly? You saw a stranger, Lord? Here? What was he like?'

Tarq turned back to Jacob, who was standing all too large and plain between them.

'This is the stranger,' said Tarq. 'This boy with the orange hair.'

Varn looked round again, and again his eyes passed over Jacob without a flicker.

'A boy with orange hair, Lord?' he echoed, mystified, and a little worried.

Tarq pointed a wavering finger.

'I see him plainly,' he said, but there was a note of doubt in his voice.

Another voice called from outside.

'A woman!' it cried. 'A blue-haired old woman! A woman, here, in the garden! Quick, quick!'

That was the voice of Firn the Librarian, that could not have been raised above a whisper for half a century. Tarq turned and hurried back out through the door.

'Quick,' said Varn, his chest still heaving. 'Tell the boy to go back to his own world. He'll have to dodge the Lords as best he can. Quick, before Tarq comes back!'

Nian gathered up his fragments of English.

'Go now,' he said urgently. 'Go to stone I saw you. I will come soon—night coming. But danger, danger. Monks not to see you.'

'They won't if I can help it,' said Jacob, fervently. 'That bloke really gave me the willies.'

'Tell him about the old woman,' said Varn.

'The old bat with blue skull go home now, too,' said Nian.

'The old . . . ' Then Jacob's eyes widened in dismay. 'What? *Nan's* here? Oh *help*! All right, I'll do my best. I just hope she hasn't duffed up too many of your monks with her handbag, that's all.'

'Go to place you here come,' said Nian, 'and I think you go home.'

Jacob was at the doorway, peering cautiously round. 'I'd better,' he said, briefly, and slipped out.

Nian and Varn stood listening.

Nothing.

'You were just so brilliant,' said Nian, softly, to Varn. 'I'd never have thought of fooling Tarq like that.'

Varn stood a little longer, alert for sounds from the garden. At last he turned to Nian.

'No,' he said, 'you wouldn't have. But you're going to have to think for yourself from now on, aren't you, little Nian. If you can.'

And he turned on his heel and walked off.

Tarq came into the schoolroom later and explained everything to them.

'In the House, the truth of everything is known,' he said. 'Our Wisdom is strong and complete. But twice each year the Lords go into the garden so we do not forget that there are still parts of the world that we do not yet understand. Still,' and here he brightened, 'the Lord Bran has been doing sterling work on earwigs, so progress is being made, my sons. Yes, indeed.'

Nian looked around at the stone walls and he marvelled that anyone could think the House was of any importance compared with the garden.

'We go also to visit the statue that stands there,' went on Tarq, 'for it is said that when it is gone, the Truth Sayer will come. And it is certainly crumbling.'

It was crumbling, all right, but it would take hundreds of years for it to crumble away altogether. So Nian couldn't possibly be the Truth Sayer.

'I believe it was the uncontrolled disorder of the garden that caused us to see visions,' Tarq explained. 'I saw a boy, and the Lord Firn saw an old woman. Which was most upsetting for him, for, having been tranquil here for so long, he had forgotten the existence of women. I hope,' he continued, mildly anxious, 'I do hope you were not alarmed.'

'We were, rather, Lord,' admitted Varn. 'But it's all right, now. We understand it all, now. Don't we, Nian?'

IIII IIII IIIIIII

Suddenly Nian was doing things for the last time. He sat through his last hour of Wisdom, he had his last lesson with Tarq, he hurled one last wooden tablet across the schoolroom. He searched himself for signs of regret as these parts of his life vanished. He was perhaps a little sorry to be leaving Tarq, for the old man had been patient, in his fashion, but he was not sorry to be leaving the House. No, he was exultantly, savagely happy to be leaving it, for it was a place of arrogance and cruelty and lies.

But he was very sorry for the pain he had caused Varn. That evening he did his best to make things as right as they could be.

'Please come with me to Jacob's world,' he said, as he washed the porridge bowls for the last time. 'I won't be able to manage without you.'

Varn heaved a sigh.

'Oh, you'll be all right,' he said. 'If that idiot Jacob can survive there, you will.'

Jacob had been casual, flippant, soft: yes, he'd been used to an easy life.

An easy life. Was that what Nian wanted?

'I wish I knew what Jacob's world is like,' he said.

Varn stacked a wooden bowl precisely in its place so as to leave no trace of himself behind.

'The Tarhun told me a story, ages ago, on the way here,' he said. 'About the time when our world was invaded.'

'Was that by people from Jacob's world?' asked Nian.

'I've no idea. But they said that when the big earthquakes started, the Lords called the Tarhun to take all their treasure out of the House in case the walls fell on it. And one of the Tarhun, a man called Snorp, was carrying a tray full of jewels into the garden when he fell off the edge of the world.'

'Jacob said he fell,' said Nian, thoughtfully. 'But he said he fell through the carpet by his fireplace.'

'Did he? He just seemed to be spitting and gargling to me. Anyway, Snorp landed up in a cave with a strange golden man who held a dirty lamp. So Snorp fought with the man for several hours until he vanquished him, and then he fought his way back to our world past a ferocious dragon that he defeated by ramming the tray into its throat so it choked on all the jewels.'

Nian listened, and felt even more doubtful.

'Jacob didn't mention dragons,' he said.

Varn nodded.

'No, of course not. That's because there won't be any,' he said. 'That part of the story will have been a lie to cover up the fact that the Tarhun had either stolen all the jewels, or else he'd fallen, sobbing with terror, at that golden man's knees (if it *was* a man, and not a little old lady or a boy), given him everything, and then run away screaming. But Nian, think: if one stupid fat Tarhun can cope with a new world, then you can. You're a hundred times more powerful than one of the Tarhun. Let's face it, you're *ten* times more powerful than *me*. Why shouldn't you manage?'

'Because next time I do something stupid I won't have you to get me out of trouble,' said Nian. 'And I'd have been finished a dozen times without your help. Anyway . . . anyway, I'll miss you.'

The fierce lines on Varn's face softened a little.

'Come to the city, then.'

'No. That's not my place. I just can't, Varn.'

Varn paused.

'And I can't go jumping into different worlds. *This* is my world. Nian, where do you really want to be? In all the worlds?'

'At home. In my father's house,' said Nian.

'And so do I. We're both exiles, Nian. That's our fate.'

Varn got suddenly to his feet and held out his hand.

'Farewell,' he said. 'I shall think of you. Go in happiness.'

Nian got up too and put his hand in Varn's.

'Farewell, Varn,' he said. 'I shall never forget how much I owe you; if I ever get the chance, I shall repay you. Go in happiness.'

And so at the end they parted with some sorrow, but no bitterness.

‖‖‖ ‖‖‖ ‖‖‖‖‖

The Lords retired early in the House of Truth. Nian and Varn lay beside one another and waited until Caul's breathing became slow and soft, for Varn would not leave him for ever under a dome of silence. Then Varn very cautiously got up, put on his clothes, and rolled up his sleeping mat. He put it away tidily. He and Nian had both been very tidy that day. They made their way down the inky corridors in silence. Nian stepped out of the House onto the path and looked up at the minuscule dots of light that were the stars. I'm going further than that, he thought; and his heart quailed at the thought of cutting himself off so absolutely from everything he knew.

'I'll fly from here,' said Varn, coming to a halt.

Nian made himself be matter-of-fact. He felt inside his tunic and brought out a piece of hartskin that he'd torn from the end of a scroll.

'This is a message to my father,' he said. 'It explains that I won't be able to come home, after all, and . . . and all that sort of thing. If you get a chance to send it I'd be grateful. If not . . . well, it won't really matter.'

Nian hadn't been able to seal his letter, so it did not say what he wished to say, but it explained that he was going far away to live a good life, and that he would not ever be able to come home. And it sent his love.

'I'll send it as soon as I can,' Varn promised. 'Though that may not be soon. Goodbye, Nian.'

'Goodbye. Go in happiness.'

Nian stood back so he would not disturb Varn's thoughts. Varn took several deep breaths to help focus his powers, and then, slowly but inevitably, he rose from the ground. He rose ten, twenty, thirty feet, until he was higher than the wall of the Outer House. Nian saw him silhouetted for a moment against the cloudy charcoal sky, and then the shape dipped and vanished behind the wall.

Nian discovered that he'd been holding his breath. He let it out in a sigh, and then, feeling inexpressibly alone, he made his way back to the sleeping room. He had no possessions, so there was nothing to take with him, nothing to wait for. He called together all his resolution and he left the House.

There was no moon, but still Nian lingered in the garden amongst the scents of flowers and wet leaves. Could he really leave all this behind?

I've got to go, he thought.

But it was with no joy but a sense of irreparable loss that he walked slowly to the statue in the middle of the garden and offered himself up to the passage between the worlds.

|||| |||| |||| ||||

There was no barrier between the worlds, but instead a void. The damp grass of the garden dropped precipitously away from under Nian's feet, and after a moment's gasping shock he found himself dropping into a chilly emptiness larger and blacker than anything he'd dreamed of. He had a moment's glimpse of the sparkling of a million diamonds and as many fiery suns. And then he was levelling out, and swooping dizzily upwards, fast, faster, until his hair tugged at his scalp and the cold struck deep into his heart.

And here was an edge to the darkness: it was flushing upwards into violet, amethyst, aquamarine. Nian was slowing down very rapidly, now, and there were shapes forming mistily around him: the shapes of a new world.

And now there was solid ground coming up to bump his feet.

Nian swallowed, and blinked around. He was in a small room cluttered with bits of furniture and ornaments.

And there by the door was Jacob, looking startled half out of his wits. The place was quiet, but the walls were vibrating faintly as if something explosive had just happened.

Jacob blew out a long breath of relief.

'*Gordon Bennett!*' he said, rather shakily. 'You nearly scared Nan to death!'

Sure enough, somewhere not far away came a rising clamour of women's voices. Nian found himself smiling, because that was a home-like noise he hadn't heard for a year.

'Hey, it's nothing to grin about,' went on Jacob, a little plaintively. 'Looming up like a ghost like that. It's enough to scare anybody, and Nan's still got the screaming abdabs from seeing all your spooky old monks. It took ages to convince her it must have been a dream.'

Nian stopped smiling. The last thing he wanted to do was offend Jacob or his grandmother.

'I hope the old bat is not scared to death,' he said, politely. 'I did not loom to scare her. I loomed coming.'

'Yeah,' said Jacob, admiringly, 'and you made a really good job of it, too. You started off sort of shadowy, and then you gradually firmed up. I think if I hadn't been expecting you *I'd* have screamed blue murder and bolted like a bat out of hell, too.'

Bat and *hell* were difficult words for Nian. *Bat* seemed to mean something diferent from *old lady*, which was how Jacob had used it before. And *hell* was very disturbing, a place full of fires and dancing men with tails and pitchforks. Nian hoped very much that it was a long way away. He looked round the room for reassurance. The walls were decorated with painted rows of brown flowers, and there was a twisty-legged table, and shelves filled with fussy models of children, or sheep, or other mythical beasts.

Nian decided there were more ugly things in that room than he had ever seen in one place in his whole life, and that included the Lords' council meetings.

But the women's voices were coming closer, now; one voice could be heard above the rest.

'*It woz a gohsst, Ei tell yoo!*'

'*Oh deer*,' said a second, worried voice. '*And in the frunt room, too. Wot an orfull shok for yoo, mum.*'

Nian grabbed hastily at his powers. The women's brains were organized differently from Jacob's, and Nian couldn't catch what they were saying. He zapped a sizzle of thought through the mustard-coloured door, and after an urgent effort managed to make their voices slot into meaning.

'*It woz probablee* Jacob messing about,' a third, younger, voice was saying, witheringly.

'You'd better hide,' said Jacob. 'Mum's fine about you staying the night, but Nan might throw a wobbly, especially if she recognizes you from just now. Quick, get down behind that chair.'

The chair was huge and dusty, and scrambling over it took a surprising amount of effort. Nian had just folded himself into the small space behind it when the door opened.

'There's nothing here now,' announced the young voice. 'What did you do with it, Jake?'

'Do with what?' asked Jacob, all injured innocence. 'I didn't do anything. I couldn't have. Could I, Nan? You should have seen it. It was all black to begin with, and then—'

'Ooh, it did give me such a shock,' said the oldest voice, which must belong to Nan. 'I thought I was seeing things. But the boy, he saw it too.'

'Oh dear,' said the worried voice (Jacob's mother, it must be). 'Did it . . . did it say anything?'

'I didn't wait to find out,' Nan told her. 'It wasn't solid, though. And I can't say it *looked* the chatty type.'

'Oh . . . oh goodness. And did it just disappear again, Jacob?'

'Well . . . it got sort of solider . . . but then I couldn't see it any more,' said Jacob, truthfully, but economically.

'But what *happened*?' demanded the young voice. 'Did it fade again, or what? Or did it go out of the door?'

'Um . . . I don't think it went out of the door,' said Jacob.

'But you must *know*!'

'It just all sort of happened,' said Jacob, rather desperately. Then, turning to the attack: 'Anyway, if you'd been helping tidy Nan's room like me then you'd have seen it for yourself.'

Nian felt the girl's mind flash with anger.

'The reason I wasn't tidying Nan's room is because it wasn't *me* who made all the mess!'

'No, no, of course it wasn't, Robyn, dear,' said Jacob's mother.

'It was over by the fireplace,' Nan went on, queru-lously. 'All pale and shimmering, with black eyes! Ooh, it made my stomach twinge.'

'Oh, what a terrible shock,' said Jacob's mother. 'I *thought* you'd been even more aggressive and difficult than usual, lately, and it must be because you've been going senile. Oh, however am I going to cope with you now?'

Nian gasped, got a lungful of dust, and nearly choked. But he must have misunderstood what Jacob's mother had just said, for Nan was answering without any sign of being offended.

'He was all thin and miserable-looking,' Nan was say-ing. 'With a green top, and trousers with straps round.'

Nian ran Jacob's mother's words through his mind again. *Wot woz hee leik?* had been the sound of them, and, come to think about it, they were all words he understood. But why had his mind received a differ-ent message altogether?

'He was a bit like a—what do you call them—a viking,' Nan was going on.

'A viking?' repeated Mum, blinking. 'Oh dear. You really *must* be quite quite totally bonkers.'

This time, the sound of Mum's words was *how garstlee*. And Nian *must* be misunderstanding her, for Nan showed no signs of going for Jacob's mother with the poker—which was what Grandy might have done, if Mother had spoken so to her.

'I suppose there *might* have been some great hero who met his death here,' said Robyn, doubtfully.

125

'He was too small to be a great hero,' Jacob pointed out.

'Oh, you're so crass, Jacob. Some small hero, then, who met his death on this very spot. In which case,' she went on, thoughtfully, 'he'll probably come back.'

Someone gave a long-suffering sniff.

'I don't think it should be allowed,' said Nan. 'Not in my front room. It's bad enough as it is, living with you lot and your lazy sponging dirty ways.'

'Oh, but I do wish we could go and live somewhere else!' said Jacob's mother.

'Silly old cow,' said Robyn.

Nian's head was spinning. The women were insulting each other at such a rate that he didn't have time to listen carefully to the sounds of their words—but they weren't shouting, or scratching each other's eyes out. What was going on?

'It's bad enough having the boy messing it up with his bits of rubbish,' said Nan, 'without—'

'It wasn't me,' put in Jacob.

'—vikings and goodness knows what else appearing out of thin air. Especially when I'm not feeling well.'

'Perhaps Jacob made some sort of projection with Grandad's old cine camera,' said Robyn, shrewdly. 'Except, of course, that he hasn't got the brains to do it.'

'Look, you go and have a sit down in the living room, Mum, and I'll be along in a minute and make you a nice cup of tea. Perhaps you'll stop nagging on and on, then,' said Jacob's mother, all respect and sympathy.

There was some retreating muttering, and then the door closed. Nian was hugely relieved, because although he knew he must be misunderstanding their speech some of the time, he'd kept expecting blood to be spilled.

'Oh, good heavens,' said Mum, weakly. 'Nan'll be having the vapours for weeks, now. What actually happened, Jacob?'

'How should I know,' said Jacob, in an injured voice.

'Because you're the only one immature enough to find this sort of thing funny!' said Robyn, so shrilly that Nian was suddenly, heart-piercingly, re-minded of his own sister, Miri, but she was far, far away beyond the end of the world.

'Oh no I—'

'Well, never mind,' said Mum, wearily. 'Let's just hope Nan doesn't see any more ghosts, that's all.' She looked round and shuddered. 'I've tried again and again to explain to Nan about the feng shui in this room. Dad's right, it's always had an odd feel to it. I do wish Nan would let me shift the furniture around.'

'Well, I hope she *does* see some more ghosts,' said Robyn. 'Then she might let me have this room for myself.'

'At least Dad isn't here, or this would be bound to bring on his nerves again,' said Mum with a sigh. 'Oh well. Come and make Nan some tea, will you, Robyn, while I see if I can find her some lavender drops to calm her down a bit.'

The door opened, and then closed again on an emptier room. Nian unfolded himself gingerly. Standing up was rather more of an effort than usual, as if the journey to this world had made him heavier.

Jacob threw himself into a chair, swung his long legs over one of the arms, and heaved a sigh.

'That was my family,' he said. 'Bossy sister, worrying mother, and nagging nan. Dad's out.'

'I have a bossy sister and a worrying mother,' said Nian, very wistful.

'But no nagging nan?' asked Jacob.

Nian thought of Grandy, soft, but tough, and always ready to listen.

'I have a nan,' he answered sadly. 'But I will never see her again.'

Jacob looked uncomfortable.

'No. Sorry,' he said. 'I forgot. It's just that Nan drives us mad. Dad's never been able to have a job for very long because he keeps being ill, so we've always had to live here with her.'

'That is not selfish of her,' pointed out Nian. And Jacob sighed again.

'Oh, but she's not come out of it badly. She has the biggest bedroom, and this room all to herself with no one else allowed to *breathe* in it, and all her meals made for her. She's generally waited on hand and foot. I mean, I'm not even allowed to put up my *Cream* poster, and that's practically an antique!'

Nian frowned a little. He seemed to be able to understand Jacob with no trouble at all, unlike the

128

others, whose speech he was obviously sometimes getting wildly wrong, but surely he couldn't have picked up the meaning of *poster* properly, because Jacob spoke as if he was complaining of some very great hardship. Nian tried to pin down Jacob's meaning, but he only ended up yawning violently. It only seemed to be the middle of the afternoon, here, which probably meant it was hours and hours before he could go to sleep. If he had anywhere to sleep.

'I suppose in your world it's night-time,' said Jacob, rather interested. 'Like yesterday. If you have a twenty-four hour day, it is, anyway. So you're suffering from sort of jet-lag. Though it's *world-lag*, really, I suppose.'

Nian nodded, because it was easier than saying anything. His vocabulary was growing fast, but Jacob kept pinging amazing new ideas at him, and Nian was beginning to feel as if he was standing in front of a pea-shooter. *Jet-lag* was staggering, especially, because it meant you must somehow be able to travel so fast you could outstrip the suns.

At least—this world must have suns. Mustn't it? Why had the vast windows got that fine netting hung over them? Was the sunlight here dangerous? Or the flies?

But that was yet another question for later.

'OK,' went on Jacob. 'We'd better get you away from the scene of the crime. Then you'll have to meet people. Mum's all right, really, but you'll have to grovel like mad to Nan.'

'What about me did you say them?'

Jacob shrugged.

'The truth. Well, some of it, anyway. I said you were a refugee, and that you'd had to leave all your family behind. Mum's really sorry for you and she said you could sleep on the airbed.'

Just for a moment Nian caught a glimpse of something really important in Jacob's words. He tried to catch what it was, but he was distracted by footsteps thumping hastily along the passage-way.

'*Hey, Jake!*' called the young voice he'd heard earlier.

'Oh no, that's Robyn!' said Jacob, leaping up and lunging towards the door. 'Quick, Nian, get back behind the—'

'Hey,' said Robyn, bursting through the door. 'Mum says do you want baked beans, or—'

She broke off and Nian found himself staring into a pair of very sharp blue eyes.

'—the *little viking*,' she said, in a low, accusing voice, 'I knew it!' And she turned back to the doorway. '*Mum!*'

Jacob began jumping up and down.

'No, don't!' he said. '*Please* don't. You've no idea how important it is. Listen to me before you tell Mum! Please, Rob! *Please!*'

Robyn snapped her head round at her brother, and Nian could almost hear the light from her eyes scorching its way into Jacob's mind.

'*Please, Rob?*' she echoed, suspiciously. 'What are you doing being so polite all of a sudden?'

Jacob was so agitated he was actually pulling at his orange hair.

'It's just fantastically important,' he said. 'Really, Rob. Truly. Just tremendously, tremendously, *tremendously* important.'

The shrewd blue eyes swept Nian from head to foot.

'All right,' she said. 'You can tell me.' Robyn turned and called back along the corridor. '*Mum! Baked beans for Jake!*'

'OK, love!'

Robyn stepped into the room and closed the door. She looked a bit older than Jacob, with dark hair and a scowl to match, but she might have been quite good-looking, in a slightly heavy sort of way, if she hadn't been wearing the same sort of coarse blue breeches and bright vest as her brother.

'This had better be worth hearing,' she said, threateningly. 'Who's this?'

Nian stepped forward, put his fingertips on his heart and bowed very respectfully. He hadn't the words for the greeting he'd have used at home, but he did his best.

'The day is nicer for seeing your eyes,' he said. 'And this world is not grisly when you are here.'

The correct answer was *I am honoured by the notice of so great a personage*, but Robyn didn't even begin to look honoured. She tossed her head, though her hair was too short to do much more than judder.

'Right,' she snapped. 'I'm telling Mum!'

'He didn't mean it!' said Jacob, hastily. 'Really he didn't. It's just that he's . . . foreign . . . that's all, and his English is a bit wonky. That's just his way of saying hello!'

131

'Come off it,' spat Robyn, with her hand on the door handle, 'no one *bows* any more. Where's he from?'

Jacob hesitated.

'You see?' said Robyn, triumphantly. 'So you needn't think you can fool *me*. He can only come from Germany or Sweden or somewhere with fair hair like that, and his accent's not spluttery enough. See, bird-brain?'

She was turning the door handle as she spoke, so Nian blurted out:

'I am from monk school!'

That stopped her. She swung round and regarded him piercingly.

'From *what*?'

Jacob clutched at his hair with bony fingers.

'It's just not fair,' he said. 'Why is there never *anywhere* I can get a bit of privacy? All right. Sit down, Nian. And, look, stop me if I say anything wrong, will you, because I don't even begin to understand this myself, properly, yet.'

||||| ||||| ||||| ||||| |

'So Nian can't go home or he'll be locked up in a monastery for the rest of his life,' Jacob finished up. 'Er . . . I think. So I asked Mum, and she says he can come to tea and stay over.'

Robyn had spent the whole of Jacob's explanation staring at Nian as if he were some unfortunate stain on the rug. Then she came over and inspected him more closely, from top to toe.

'Don't go near the fireplace,' warned Jacob. 'You might get sucked into Nian's world!'

Robyn hastily stepped back, then she hesitated.

'I'd quite like to see it—if it exists,' she said. 'What do you have to do to get there?'

'I not like, you not like,' said Nian, too urgently to think about ordering his words. 'And if they see you they come too and then they sort out me!'

'Oh *crikey*,' said Jacob, in heartfelt tones. 'Do you mean that your spooky old monks may follow you here? That's *all* we need.'

'But we can't have *monks* storming the house on a kidnap mission!' said Robyn, sharply. 'And we can't have people sucked into a different world whenever anyone tries to dust the mantelpiece, either.'

'No,' said Nian, but still carefully polite. 'But soon the worlds will . . . will . . . there will not be a door, and the people will not be sucked.'

Jacob was staring at his sister in amazement.

'You mean you actually *believe* all this?' he asked. 'You really believe all that stuff about different worlds? And ghostly monkeries? *Why?*'

'Well, for one thing, because you've been cleaning Nan's room,' pointed out Robyn. 'That's only slightly more likely than a visitor from another world. And there are Nian's shoes, as well: you can't buy anything like that in the shops this year. And boys with such long hair aren't common, either.'

'That's a thought,' said Jacob. 'He'll need different clothes before Nan sees him. And a haircut, too.'

Robyn looked at Nian the way Mother used to regard slime-lice in cabbages.

'We'll have to get him up to our room,' she said. 'We'll probably be able to find some clothes that'll do. He's small, though. How old is he?'

Nian felt a spurt of annoyance. They were talking about him as if he were unable to think for himself. But he had been chosen to be a Lord of Truth, and he was possessed of more power than either of them dreamed of.

'I am small,' he said, with dignity, 'but I have much wizard.'

But Jacob and Robyn only snorted furtively, perhaps with laughter, and ignored him.

134

'I'll make sure the coast's clear,' announced Robyn. 'I'll sneeze when it is, OK? But tread quietly, for goodness' sake, Nian, or Nan'll be on at us again for wearing out the stair carpet.'

The sneeze, when it came, was almost too realistic to trust, but Nian followed Jacob into a narrow passage that smelt of damp. They went quietly up some stairs made even steeper by the heaviness of Nian's legs, and along to a door at the end of a small landing.

It led into a tiny cupboard-like room, most of which was taken up by a large wooden frame upon which were spread two quilts, one above the other.

Jacob groped under the quilt frame and brought out a ladder.

'Get up on the top bunk,' he said. 'There's not room to breathe, otherwise.'

The quilt was fantastically springy, but the ceiling was hardly high enough to allow Nian to sit up.

Robyn, below him, was rummaging in the cupboards that lined the opposite wall.

'You'll have to be smart if Nan's not going to hate you,' she said. 'The trouble is that Jacob's the scruffiest person in the universe . . . but look, here's a shirt. And you'd better wear a tie, as well.'

'On a Friday evening?' asked Jacob, doubtfully, scratching his head.

'Nan'll like it. He can wear this one she got you for your birthday.'

'Well, *I'm* never wearing it,' said Jacob, darkly.

'I will be glad to please your nan,' said Nian, feeling guilty about her again, for she was a grandmother, and so must be at least a little like Grandy. Then he pushed away that thought, because remembering Grandy made his insides feel hollow.

'Here we are,' said Robyn. 'Put them on. I'll be back in a minute.'

Jacob's shirt was made of fabric as sheer as a woman's headcloth—except for the collar and cuffs, which were exceedingly stiff and uncomfortable. It had little buttons in the silliest places. But at least the tie caused him no problems, though the patterned silk reminded him of Varn. And fried eggs.

Nian was securing the knot when Robyn slid back into the room. She was holding a pair of silver scissors. Nian looked at them with respect, for they were just about the first really useful things he'd seen in that world.

Jacob's jaw dropped when he saw them.

'Nan's cutting-out scissors!' he breathed. 'She'll go bonkers!'

'So?' said Robyn, rolling her eyes. 'The worst she can do is launch a new attempt to nag me to death. Come on down, Nian: you're going to have to have your pigtails cut off if you want to look respectable.'

'I am glad to have them cut off,' Nian told her as he climbed down. 'They mean I am a monk. I will be glad when the disgusting grisly things are gone.'

'Good,' said Robyn, snipping the scissors with

slightly alarming relish. 'We'll soon have you looking as if you have lived here all your life.'

'Not if he's wearing my tie round his waist, he won't,' pointed out Jacob.

The correct way to wear a tie, Nian discovered, was even more intricately annoying and baffling than the buttons on his shirt. Even Jacob couldn't do it up properly without standing behind Nian and breathing down his neck—and in the end all it did was hang down in front of him like a halter and make his collar feel even stiffer than before.

Robyn enjoyed cutting Nian's hair. Nian sat on the up-turned bin and tried not to think about Mother, for Robyn frowned and squinted and pulled at his hair in just the same way. But it was worth it, just to hear his squat pigtails thump down onto the mat. Jacob reclined on the bottom bunk to watch and kept saying things like 'It's too short on the other side, now,' or 'I wouldn't let Rob's fingers anywhere near my hair,' or 'Are you sure you should have started this?' while Robyn hissed with annoyance.

'There!' said Robyn, at last. 'Perfect. What do you think, Jake?'

'It's all right,' said Jacob, after a pause.

'Which is high praise, from you. Nian, look in the mirror.'

The mirror was brighter and clearer even than the washing trough on a sunny day at home. Nian looked at himself and recoiled. He looked *old*; old, and starved to the bone. He'd spent very nearly a year in

137

the House of Truth, and every week had left its mark. He looked . . . he looked as if he'd never laughed in his life.

How long was it since he'd laughed properly, really been carefree?

'*Robyn! Jacob! Tea's ready!*'

'Coming!' yelled Jacob and Robyn together.

Nian tore his gaze away from the haunted stranger in the mirror and stepped aside so Robyn could gather up the corners of the mat and tip his cast-off hair into the bin.

'I'll go down,' said Robyn. 'Jake, you find Nian a pair of trousers. Oh, and Nian, don't *bow* to Nan, whatever you do. And hurry up!'

'Dead bossy,' commented Jacob, but not until the door had closed behind her. 'Here, try these.'

The trousers were easy. There was an ingenious metal tag that plaited the front opening closed.

'OK,' said Jacob. 'Just say "*Hello, Mrs Rush*" to Mum and Nan. Otherwise I should shut up if I were you. Your English is a bit wonky, and you might accidentally insult someone.'

Nian followed Jacob back down the dark stairs. This house was so low and cramped it was almost like the hen house at home; but there was a spicy smell wafting along the passageway that set his mouth watering in a way it hadn't done for a year.

'Mum,' said Jacob, pushing open a door, 'Mum, it's still all right if Nian comes to tea, isn't it?'

There was an old woman sitting at a table with Robyn,

but Nian looked first at the woman who must be Jacob's mother. She had straggly colourless hair, and she was too worn and worried to be pretty. But she looked kind.

He found he envied Jacob so much he almost hated him.

'Hello, Nian,' said Mum, smiling.

'A visitor?' said the old woman who was sitting next to Robyn at the table that took up very nearly the whole room. 'When I'm not feeling well? I did think I might have a say in who gets his feet under the table, Susan.'

'Oh, but you'd have made such a dreadful fuss about it, and you'd have said he couldn't come,' said Mum, soothingly.

Nian felt the familiar double-speak bump as Jacob's mum said this, as the meaning came into his head somehow separately from the words: *Oh, but ei did-dunt wont too wurree yoo.* It was horribly disorientating, and disappointing, too, because he'd thought this had stopped happening.

Nan looked Nian up and down and didn't seem to think much of him.

'Hello, Mrs Rush,' said Nian, as politely as he could.

But Nan stiffened at the sound of his voice.

'Is he *foreign*?' she asked, outraged, and the rest of the family cringed.

'We've only got fish fingers,' asked Jacob's mum, hastily. 'I hope you don't mind.'

Fish fingers was puzzling—fish had fins in Nian's world—but they smelt wonderful.

139

'You are very good,' said Nian, gratefully, sitting down. He used the time while Mum was bringing in the plates to worry about table manners. His knife had no point, so did you pick up the golden sticks of— whatever—with the tiny fork?

Mum came hurrying in with the last plate.

'Don't let it get cold,' she said. 'Nian, would you like some ketchup?'

'Oh no,' said Nian, hastily, for the word conjured up an image of something like congealed blood.

He managed by copying Mum, who sat opposite him. It was easy once he knew how you held the fork, but he was still the last to finish.

'I hope it was all right,' said Mum, reaching for his plate.

If only Nian had been able to answer in his own language he would have told her that it had been a delicious and glorious feast, a landmark in a year of greyness and hunger.

'It was very brilliant,' he said earnestly. 'I liked it very very.'

'He's not *German*, is he?' asked Nan. Jacob choked.

'No, Nan,' said Robyn. 'Nian's never even been to Germany. Have you, Nian?'

'Never, Mrs Rush.'

Nan sniffed grudgingly. Nian kept trying not to stare at her hair. It was pale blue, which was quite peculiar enough, but it also seemed really *rigid*, as if it had been starched.

Nian accepted the offer of a glass of milk after the meal, but it tasted so odd that he rather shuddered to think what sort of an animal it'd come from. He sipped it politely and stifled a yawn that made his ears pop.

'So where *are* you from, Nian?' asked Mum, kindly, sitting herself down.

But he was suddenly too tired to work out a proper answer.

'Thion,' he said.

'It's up in the mountains,' put in Robyn, without batting an eyelid. 'Hardly anyone's heard of it. There was this terrible disaster and Nian had to leave.'

'Oh, what a terrible thing,' said Mum. 'Oh, how dreadful. And how long will it be until you can go home again, Nian?'

For ever.

'I can never go home, Mrs Rush.'

'Never?'

Nan shifted irritably in her seat.

'Half the countryside under concrete, and the country's still taking in immigrants!'

Jacob looked mortified, but Robyn only glared.

'You are a silly cow, Nan,' she said, but fortunately in the giddying double-speak of words and meaning, *yoo needunt wurree, nan* was all that came out in her words. 'Nian was the only one who got away.'

Nian was glad Robyn had said that last bit. It gave him an excuse for looking as unhappy and lost as he felt.

$$\cancel{||||}\ \cancel{||||}\ \cancel{||||}\ \cancel{||||}||$$

Nan was old, and therefore worthy of the deepest respect, but still, Nian was glad to get away from her. Luckily, this seemed to be expected. Nan sat down in the back room to do something called watching telly (which was an interesting thing, but not, as far as Nian could understand it, important); Mum went into the kitchen to do ironing; and Jacob and Robyn and Nian wandered out into the hall.

'We don't go in the front room, usually,' explained Robyn. 'Nan declares a major crime incident in there if we so much as dent one of the cushions. Anyway, it's got foul wallpaper. And it's really creepy with all those china eyes everywhere, as well. Isn't it, Jake?'

'Er . . . yeah,' said Jacob. 'Yeah, it can be a bit spooky, sometimes.'

'Mind you,' went on Robyn, 'Nan's a complete witch. She's enough to spook anyone.'

Nian blinked with surprise.

'Mrs Rush is a witch?' he asked. There was no such thing as witches in his own world. Probably.

'No, not really,' said Jacob, reassuringly.

'No,' snorted Robyn. 'Otherwise we could get her burned at the stake.'

Nian, shaken, shrugged himself into the coat Jacob threw him. It hadn't occurred to him that people with powers might be persecuted so horribly here. He shuddered, remembering how close he'd got to telling Jacob and Robyn about his own powers, and followed the others out through the front door.

The sky in this world was grey, like a heavy blanket of smoke. There was a superb road without a single wheel-rut anywhere (that was grey, too) . . . and, hang on, there was something really huge coming along very fast towards them. It was a thing like a haystack-sized beetle, with armoured plates and fierce white eyes, and it was *growling*.

The air was heavy in that world, but Nian was over the wall behind them in a matter of seconds.

The thing must be some sort of enormous insect, but it was going so fast Nian hardly had time to . . .

. . . *vroooooooom* . . .

. . . and then it was hurtling away again.

Nian stood up again, even more shaken than before. Jacob and Robyn were looking round in all directions.

'There he is,' exclaimed Jacob, at last.

'Oh, good *grief*,' said Robyn. 'Nian, *what* are you doing in Miss Sprogett's front garden?'

The growly thing had apparently not been a beetle at all, but some sort of oxless wagon.

'Look, here's another one,' said Jacob. 'See? It's got a driver.'

143

'And door-handles,' pointed out Robyn, witheringly, rolling her eyes.

It took some nerve to stand and watch the thing rumbling towards them, but it was true, there was a man sitting inside. The wagon growled past and away, leaving Nian enveloped in the stink of the bluish wind it was blowing out of its backside.

'See?' said Jacob. 'They're not dangerous.'

'Yes they are,' Robyn corrected him, smartly. 'So don't try walking out in front of one, Nian. OK?'

Nian walked along warily between them. This was a most peculiar place. For one thing there were no mountains anywhere: there were only houses, which were grey, like the road and the sky, and of quite amazing ugliness.

'Where here can I find work?' Nian asked.

'Oh, you won't need to work,' Robyn told him. 'We have special places that look after children with no homes. You'll be able to go into care.'

Nian shook away the image *care* put in his mind. *Care* seemed to be a sort of prison; a lonely place filled with people who were not allowed to love each other.

'I do not want to go into care,' said Nian, firmly.

'Oh, it might be all right,' said Jacob, vaguely. 'And anyway,' he admitted, 'I'm not sure there's anything else you'll be able to do.'

'I can work,' pointed out Nian.

'Oh no you can't,' said Robyn. 'No one here is allowed to work until they're grown up.'

Nian was filled with disbelief and dismay. When his cousins had been orphaned, after the storm, they had chosen to stay in their own village. One had found work with a weaver, and the other at the inn. Nian's family visited them, or sent them presents, all the time. Their lives were not easy, exactly, but they were theirs.

Surely, however this world worked, there must be some farmer somewhere who needed help.

'Where does food come from?' Nian asked, still lacking many words.

Jacob jerked his red head at a building across the road.

'In there,' he said. 'Come on. Mum gave me some money.'

Robyn pushed open the glass door in the vast glass wall. (Glass? Why glass?? Glass was *stupid* for a door or a wall. And who could blow a pane that big? A giant? Nian began to wonder if he was losing his grip on reality: after all, it was six hours past his bedtime, and the heavy air of that world was exhausting to walk through in itself.)

The food place was bizarre: as soon as Nian took a step inside, thousands of reds and oranges and every other colour leapt screaming into his brain so that he had to shake his head to clear it. He'd longed for colour when he was shut up in the cold whiteness of the House, and here it was in abundance: almost more colour than he could bear.

He followed Robyn up an aisle. What sort of food did all these boxes contain? Was it *grown* in the boxes?

145

And if it was, who planted the seed? Someone must have done.

'I'll get some crisps,' said Jacob, picking up a metal cushion. Except that it couldn't be metal at all, because it was blown up like a bladder. 'We can eat them in the park,' he said.

Robyn tutted.

'Friday night, and I'm going to sit in the park with my little brother and an alien,' she muttered. 'Ah well. It's not as if I could go anywhere decent in these jeans, anyway.'

The *park* was a field with broken benches in it. Nian perched himself on an intact plank and felt glad to be still. His mind had been zapped by so many extraordinary images over the last few hours: Jacob's crowded house, the superb roads, the oxless wagons, the glass-doored store . . .

'The trouble is, Nian *looks* really young,' said Robyn. 'How old are you, Nian?'

Nian didn't have the words for that, so he held up his hands.

'Eleven,' said Jacob, confidently. Then: 'Er . . . six,' he went on, baffled, as Nian rearranged his fingers.

'Yes,' agreed Nian. 'Eleven and six.'

'*Eleven and six*?' echoed Robyn. 'But that's not an age, that's the price of Nan's wedding hat!'

Nian, irritated, couldn't see what the trouble was. He *was* eleven and six. How else could you count your age, except by the circuits of the suns?

But perhaps you never got to see the suns, here.

'Oh well,' said Jacob, philosophically. 'I don't suppose it really matters. Have a crisp.'

The crisp seemed to be covered in sand, but the others were eating them. Nian bit into one dubiously . . . and actually groaned with rapture. Meat, salt, spices: oh, fantastic, fantastic, fantastic. Hope flowed into him anew. This place was crammed with people—he could see hundreds of houses from where he sat—so surely he could find someone who needed him.

He had his powers, too. They would have to be secret powers, because of the burnings at the stake, but they would be useful for all sorts of things, like getting through locked doors. So he could easily help himself to a night's lodging here and there. These people were not exactly stupid, but they were as set in their ways as mountain goats, and he could surely out-wit them.

Robyn shivered.

'It's getting chilly,' she said. 'Let's go home.'

At the edge of the park was a low building that did not seem quite like a house. Nian peered in as they went past.

'Why are there no people in that house?' he asked.

'Oh, that's the surgery. There's never anyone there at night,' Robyn said.

That sounded promising. Nian sent out a delicate thought to search the building. Inside were several comfortable padded benches, and a water-supply in nearly every room.

So how did you get in?

147

Nian set his mind to probe the jagged hole in the door handle . . .

. . . and *something started screaming.*

Jacob jumped so high he had time to look wildly round in all directions before he hit the ground again.

'Wuk!' said Robyn. '*Run!*'

There was a bush across the road that was big enough to hide behind.

'*Woh!*' said Jacob. 'What set *that* off?'

Nian was panting too much to speak. He threw a thought across the road to the red box on the wall that was screaming on and on and on and . . .

. . . *off!*

The box melted with a *phizz* and a *spickle,* but Nian just concentrated on taking in enough air to stay alive.

'Moronic things,' gasped Robyn.

Nian swallowed, and managed to speak.

'What was it?'

'The burglar alarm. They're always going off.'

Nian nodded. In future he would have to check for alarms before he explored a lock.

'Will people come?' he asked.

'Well, I'm not waiting to find out,' said Jacob.

They set off at a brisk pace, but using his powers had left Nian as tired as he had ever been, now.

'You OK?' asked Jacob, jogging backwards.

'I am coming,' said Nian, though suddenly he wasn't really sure how much further he could walk. He really needed to stop: to stop walking, but even more than that to set his mind free for a while of everything in this strange strange world.

'Come *on* then!' called Robyn. 'I'm getting cold.'

'You're *not* OK, are you?' said Jacob. 'What's up?'

Nian forced his mind to find some words to explain.

'This world . . . it is full of many weird things,' Nian admitted.

Jacob looked round. The place seemed to have an infinite supply of grey skies, and grey roads, and grey houses. It somehow contrived to be utterly dull, and yet utterly, brain-stabbingly, peculiar.

'We'll go home the back way,' he suggested. 'It's quieter, and not that much further. Come on, it's just down here.'

Nian plodded after Jacob and Robyn along a path that ran between knitted wire fences (*knitted* fences? *Knitted?*). After a while the path turned along beside a field; then Nian's feet came to a halt, not out of exhaustion, but out of sheer and utter amazement.

There were . . . he looked away, blinked several times, and looked again . . . but there *were*. Dotted about here and there in front of him in a field. And— look! Look! Jumping about!

A little way away Robyn was saying *what's up now?* in an annoyed voice, but Nian couldn't even think of replying. He was too busy being amazed.

Jacob jogged questioningly back to him.

Nian pointed a trembling finger. He didn't think he could have managed a word in any language at that moment.

149

Jacob looked.

'Er . . . sheep,' he said.

It was true, then.

'Sheep,' Nian repeated, filled with awe. 'And . . . and *small* sheeps.'

Jacob scratched his red head.

'Lambs,' he suggested.

'Lambs,' whispered Nian, in wonder.

Lambs! There were *lambs*, really *lambs*, in the field in front of him. He wondered rather wildly if there might be a dragon in the next field, or a griffon, or a wortle, or an ostrich.

'What's happening?' demanded Robyn, coming up.

'It's the sheep. I think they've sort of gone down big,' explained Jacob, in some bemusement.

Nian shook himself back into English.

'In my world sheep are not real,' he explained, and he realized that the milk at tea must have been *sheep's* milk. No wonder it had tasted funny. But good. Yes, it had tasted good. On the whole. 'Do the sheep really give clothes?' he asked, still hardly able to believe the legends might be true. 'And sing?'

'Sort of,' said Jacob. 'Their coats get cut off in the summer and made into jumpers. Like this one.'

Nian felt Jacob's jumper respectfully. The thread was coarse, but it would be warm.

And he suddenly found that he knew what he was going to do with his life.

'I shall be sheep man,' he said, just tremendously excited. 'That is what I shall do.'

Robyn and Jacob looked at one another.

'A shepherd?' said Robyn. 'That's not going to pay much.'

'I do not want much,' said Nian, still full of wonder and delight.

'I suppose it might be quite cool, really,' said Jacob, rather doubtfully. 'That is the sort of job kids do. You know, mucking out, and stuff. And I think Mum said the bloke who owns the sheep comes into the café sometimes.'

'*Do* you muck out sheep?' asked Robyn, with distaste. 'You'd probably have to wear wellies and overalls.'

'Yes,' said Nian, happily. 'I shall like it all very very.'

He hardly noticed how tired he was during the rest of the journey home. Sheep. His blood ran hot with excitement. To be a farmer would be all he could ask for, but to be a *shepherd* . . .

'I suppose it *is* sort of exciting, if you've never believed in them before,' said Robyn, grudgingly.

'Yeah. Sort of like coming across a field of unicorns,' agreed Jacob. 'Hey, Nian! Did you have *unicorns* where you lived?'

'Almost never,' said Nian, frowning. 'That was more towards . . . towards the place where the moon goes down.'

Then it was Jacob's and Robyn's turn to be amazed.

'To the west?' said Robyn. 'Really? Unicorns?'

Nian nodded.

'Grisly disgusting beasts,' he said, and went back to thinking about sheep.

Nian woke the next morning on the peculiar yielding bumpiness of the thing Jacob called an air-bed. It was like lying on floating boulders.

He lay and listened to the unfamiliar songs of the birds: his first new day in this new world.

It was a weird, alarming, miraculous, fascinating place. The people seemed kind enough, on the whole, (as long as they didn't know you had powers); and though Nan was grumpy and difficult, she was no worse than Fat Annis who ran the village inn. And Mr Rush, Jacob's father, who'd come home just as Nian was at long last going to bed, had been casual and friendly almost to a shocking degree for the head of the house.

But it was clear that Nian wouldn't be able to stay here with Jacob much longer: no one had actually told him he must leave, but everybody seemed to be assuming he'd be going that morning.

Well, he would ask Mum to introduce him to the sheep man, and he would spend the nights in the surgery for now. Jacob would probably help with food until Nian was paid. He'd have everything he needed, then.

The daylight streamed dustily through a crack in the curtains, but there was no sound of movement from anywhere in the house. Robyn and Jacob were both still hummocked under their quilts. Did people sleep through the daylight in this world? Nian had gone to sleep with the suddenness of someone falling down a well, but he'd been half-aware of people stepping over him as he slept, and he rather thought the others had stayed up long into the night.

Nian sat himself up cautiously and wriggled his legs free of his sleeping bag.

He made his way down the strip of mouldy-looking rug on the stairs and along to the door at the darker end of the hall. There were saucepans on the shelf here, so this must be the kitchen. But there was no glowing fire, and no smell of new bread, and no one to welcome him.

This is not my world, he realized, with a piercing draught of dismay. But he brushed that thought away. It would be all right. He was going to be a shepherd. Just think what Father would say . . .

. . . except that Father would never know.

Never.

Nian quietly tried another door, and found what he was looking for. Jacob had shown him how to make a waterfall come down to flush out the privy—brilliant, that was, almost like magic—but it took a little while to work out how to fill the sink to wash his hands. Heating the water was easy: just one hard-flung piece of Wisdom, and steam was rising and misting the mirror. Nian came out with a feeling of accomplishment. There was still no sign of anyone else being awake, so he turned the key in the back door.

Outside was a strip of pale rock crumbled at the edges with weeds, and a tarred fence. To the right was a barn with a square door that took up the whole wall. Nian stepped out, walked along to the corner of the house—and suddenly felt at home.

The back garden here was nothing like the garden of the House, or the vegetable garden at home, but there was a tiny pond, and a small patch of rough grass surrounded by bushes.

He stepped onto the grass, ignoring the clench of the icy dew on his bare feet, and went over to the pond. The water proved to be inhabited by a multitude of wriggling red worms and tiny jerky things. Just like home.

'Hello!'

Jacob's mum was waving at him from the kitchen window.

'You're up early,' she said. 'Come and have some breakfast.'

Nian left the pond creatures to wriggle away by themselves and made his way back to the house. He wasn't hungry, because last night's meal had been more than a whole day's food in the House, but that didn't mean he was going to refuse anything.

The kettle was bubbling as he went in: a homelike sound.

'What will you have to eat?' asked Jacob's mum.

Nian hadn't a clue.

'What you have,' he said.

'Well, I have muesli, but you're welcome to whatever you like. Toast and cornflakes?'

Toast was just about the first food word Nian had understood. But it was made in a box. You put slices of bread in it, and they popped up all by themselves when they were done. *Cornflakes* were eaten from a bowl. They tasted wonderful, but they took ever such a lot of swallowing.

'Oh, good grief, you're eating them without milk! (*Errr . . . dohnt yoo hav milk on them?*)' said Mum, startled.

Nian, with his mouth full of honey-flavoured gravel, went scarlet.

'Milk would be very,' he said, weakly, once he'd finally emptied his mouth.

'Here we are, then,' said Mum, pouring the too-white liquid that must be sheep's milk into his bowl from a square frosted bottle. 'But I'm afraid you didn't find the air-bed very comfortable. Or do you usually get up at dawn?'

'I usually get up at dawn,' said Nian.

'Well, it's nice to have some company at breakfast,' said Mum, crunching away happily at a bowl of milk-swimming sweepings. 'You won't catch my two getting up at five in the morning. And I wouldn't, either, if it wasn't for work. It's only in a café, you know, but we get a lot of passing trade in for breakfast. And it keeps the wolf from the door.'

That surprised Nian, because he wouldn't have said this was wolf country. At home, wolves lived in the high forests. But then again, although *wolf* was a word he knew, somehow Mum was not quite thinking about wolves. And they'd gone out yesterday without bothering about them—and what about the sheep? Nian tried to get some words together to ask if the outside was safe for one person, alone, but Mrs Rush was grabbing a coat, and a bag that was surely too small to hold anything useful, and making for the door.

Nian washed up, and was stacking the clean dishes when Mr Rush staggered in. He was yawning and gummy-eyed, but he said hello, and even managed a bleary sort of smile.

'Yeah,' he said. 'Er . . . nice of you to wash up.'

'I was awake,' said Nian, as an excuse. Then he realized something. 'But I did not wash . . . *that*.' And he pointed at the box that had made the toast.

Mr Rush's smile withered slightly.

'Yeah, well, that's good, really,' he said. 'Great, actually. Because you'd probably have ended up killing yourself. And setting the house on fire, as well.'

Nian stared at him, appalled.

'I didn't know,' he said, humble and bewildered. If you could set a house on fire in this world by pouring water on a box, what else might he do?

Witnessing Mr Rush eat his breakfast was deeply depressing. Father ate breakfast in his Hall with his people around him—a hearty breakfast, to keep them all going during a day in the fields. Surely that was much more civilized than this getting up one at a time and going out without so much as a farewell. Mr Rush was unshaven, and his hair was greasy and unkempt: not like the leader of the family at all. Nian, ashamed for him, was rather relieved when Mr Rush moved towards the privy.

Nian washed up again. In this world water was stored somewhere behind tubes in the wall. Nian avoided the red-labelled one in case it was dangerous, and wondered how it could work.

Mr Rush came back still unshaven, and still with the same shifty look in his eyes.

'I usually spend some time meditating in the garden before anyone else gets up,' he said.

Time meditating seemed to be a bit like an Hour of Thought, but even so, Nian could really see the attraction of it. This world was such a busy, noisy place that it was enough, as Jacob had said, to give you the screaming abdabs.

'Yeah,' went on Mr Rush, thoughtfully. 'I'm sure it helps. Blossom—she works in the Health Food Shop—she says it endows you with Higher Powers.'

'And . . . does no one want to burn you at the stake?' asked Nian, rather confused, for as far as he could tell Mr Rush had the powers of a new-born mouselet.

'What? Oh, no. No. No, that was stopped hundreds of years ago. No, people are very respectful of spirituality, now. Mostly. Sometimes. And I do find it helps my health, you know?'

Mr Rush did not look healthy, for his face was horribly pale against the black of his stubble. Nian cast a gentle waft of Wisdom at him, searching for the illness that kept him from working to provide for his family.

The pulse of power passed evenly through Mr Rush's thin pale body, but it didn't snag on anything as it went. Nian paused, puzzled, and then tried again: a delicate, searching Thought.

But there was nothing, except for a sore toe, a slightly rotting tooth, and an uneasy stomach caused by trying to digest a highly spiced piece of meat too late last night.

Nian was even more puzzled than before, but he called up a pulse of healing anyway. The Lords had to sit in silence to keep up a battle against infection, or to trap a broken bone in splints, but Nian could heal people without even thinking about it. That was the one sort of Wisdom he could do—though according to Grodan he did it in completely the wrong way.

When Nian checked, he found that Dad's sore places were beginning to heal already.

Perhaps I will be able to help many people, he thought. Like Grandy does.

He asked to be shown the garden.

Mr Rush seemed a little happier outside. The garden was hardly bigger than the house, and it was overgrown and neglected, but Mr Rush showed Nian round every inch.

'Hairy bittercress,' he said, fondly. 'My nettle corner. And this is cuckoo flower. It likes this boggy bit where the overflow leaks. And this,' went on Mr Rush, proudly, 'is my woodland patch. All those ash-trees are self-set.'

They looked more like weeds than trees: a strip of straggly plants and rubble.

'Why do you have it?' Nian asked, but respectfully.

'Well . . . to help the environment, really.'

Environment seemed to mean the same as *world*. Nian looked at the plot of scrubby weeds. He couldn't imagine what good it could be. It wasn't pretty, and it certainly wasn't a crop.

'I can't understand,' he said.

'Well,' said Mr Rush, blinking as if the light hurt his eyes, 'you see, there are so many people in the world that there isn't enough space for all the plants and animals. So we have to look after everything we can.'

This was so unlike the way the Lords thought that Nian was quite shocked.

'Do many people look after everything?' he asked, wondering if this explained the wolves.

'Oh yes. More and more people. We've lost so much, you know—the dodo, the giant sloth, the sabre-toothed tiger, the elephant bird—and now the ice-caps are melting, as well.'

'And . . . is that bad?' asked Nian, bewildered, for at home snow and ice were enemies, and he certainly felt no inclination to meet either a sabre-toothed tiger or a giant sloth himself.

Mr Rush rubbed at his unshaven chin.

'Well . . . it sort of upsets the way things fit together, I think,' he said. 'I saw a programme about it once. It's all really really important.' He sighed, and looked at the metal disc he wore strapped to his wrist. 'I'd better take my mother her tea,' he said. 'Stay out here if you want to, Nian: it's a good place to be peaceful.'

It was a good place. The sky was clear, today, but it was a different colour to that of his own world, a warmer, more velvety blue. And now the leading sun—quite a small yellow one—had come up, it had lit the rough grass with beads of gold. Nian sat down on the path and let the sun warm him. He was glad to be still. He'd hated the quiet of the House of Truth, but this world was so full of bustle and chatter and argument that his head kept feeling as if it might explode.

So it was an effort not to scowl when he heard the back door open again.

'Sleep well?' asked Jacob, cheerfully, his red hair clashing violently with everything.

'Yes,' said Nian.

Jacob looked even more pleased with himself.

'Yes. Yes, I've been perfectly comfortable on an air-bed myself,' he announced, as if he'd invented them. 'Must be better than sleeping on one of those hairy mats you have in your spooky House.'

'No,' said Nian, still irritable at being interrupted yet again. 'Mats are better.'

'Come off it! They were like doormats.'

'A mat is perfectly comfortable to me,' said Nian. 'In my world all have mats. My family, the monks—all

160

have comfortable mats, not your-world beds which go up and down and up and down like—' He stopped, frustrated, lacking the word.

'A yoyo?' suggested Jacob. 'A pea in a whistle? A pogo-stick?'

Nian's head was spinning with all these words, and none of them was the one he wanted. He pushed his legs out in front of him and pulled at imaginary oars.

'A boat,' said Jacob.

Nian nodded, exhausted. He rested his head on his knees and almost wished he was back with Varn and the Lords.

And now here was someone else.

'What's up with Nian?' asked Robyn.

'He was all right until he saw you.'

'You, more like. I expect all those carrots are giving him stomach-ache.'

And suddenly Nian couldn't stand any more. He nearly screamed at them, but then he had a better idea and he just stopped understanding their English. At once their words dissolved into meaningless jabbering and Nian felt himself relax. I must do this more often, he thought. Robyn was getting as mad as a tiger-wasp: she was going to lash out in a minute.

Nian braced himself; but the squabble never got that far. It was ended instead by someone inside the house.

Someone screaming.

IIII IIII IIII IIII IIII

They all stopped and stared at each other. Then the front door banged.

'What the . . . ' breathed Jacob, but Robyn was already halfway back to the house. Nian scrambled heavily to his feet, grabbed hastily at the waistband of his sleeping leggings, which was made of some dangerous stretchy stuff, and followed her as fast as he could.

Nan was sitting on the bottom stair. Everyone was tending to her. Mr Rush was holding her hand, Robyn was undoing the top button of her violently flowery blouse, and Jacob was fanning them all with a hat.

Nian passed a swift pulse of Wisdom through Nan to find out what was wrong. He found old age, as he'd expected, and also much loneliness and disappointment and—yes, there—a large open sore inside her, so tender that he winced away as he touched it with his mind.

'What happened?' Robyn was asking.

'I don't know,' replied Dad. 'I was upstairs doing some chanting. Er . . . have you got any ideas, Jake?'

Dad failed not to sound suspicious.

'I was out in the garden with Nian and Rob,' said Jacob, injured. 'Why do I always get blamed for everything?'

Nian called up another pulse of healing. He could do nothing about the loneliness or disappointment or old age, but he could heal the ulcer that was being burnt and enlarged by the acid in her stomach.

'*Ooooh*,' said Nan, dramatically. '*Ooooh*.'

'I hope you're not dying,' said Mr Rush, worriedly; or, at least, that was what Nian heard his mind say, though by now he was not surprised that the actual words bumped along with a completely different meaning: *Speek too mee, Mum*. 'I'd get very stressed if you turned out to be dying. (*Ar yoo orl reit?*)'

'Perhaps we should get her a drink,' suggested Robyn.

Nian went and got a cup of water, and by the time he got back Nan was taking more notice.

'Oh my,' she gasped. 'I saw something else. Oh, I think I must be going barmy, John!'

She really meant this, so Nian, alarmed, checked her mind: but it was really no more peculiar than before, and the ulcer was already beginning to heal.

Jacob was scratching his red head, and Mr Rush was looking even more bewildered and helpless than usual.

'It's probably stress, Mum,' he said. 'Terrible thing, stress can be. I could get you a crystal of tranquillity from the Health Food Shop, if you like. They're on special offer.'

But that only enraged her.

'You and your blessed crystals! It'll take more than that to sort this out. Help me up, then!'

They hoisted Nan to her feet and got her established on a chair. Nian suspected her of relishing the attention more than strictly necessary, but it turned out she'd had every excuse for screaming. Nian felt like screaming, himself.

'Ooh, I saw another man,' she said. 'Another man, in the front room. Oh, it did give me a shock.'

Nian's heart jumped with alarm. Another man? But did that mean someone had followed him down the passageway? But who could it be? No one should be going into the garden of the House for months, now; and it wasn't as if anyone would know which way he'd gone.

'What sort of a man?' demanded Robyn.

'Ooh, a great tramp,' said Nan. 'Fat. Scruffy. All in red. Some sort of dirty hippy, I should say. With a blooming ponytail.'

Nian's heart bumped violently. *Tarhun!* That man must be one of the Tarhun, and somehow he must have blundered down the passageway. But what would one of the Tarhun have been doing in the garden? And why was the passageway still open? The scroll said a few days at most, and it'd been more than that. And where was the blasted Tarhun now? Oh help, oh help, oh *help*.

Robyn was giving him a black look, but Mr Rush was wrinkling his brow.

'Sue mentioned that you saw a—a spirit-figure yesterday,' he said. 'Do you think this was the same as that?'

Nan gave a snort. She was gaining strength by the minute as her ulcer healed, and she had got what had happened clear in her mind, now.

'Nothing like it,' she snapped. 'That was a weedy-looking thing, like something from that dream I had. This one was solid. Some nasty vagrant, I should think. Why, I could smell the beer on him. Goodness knows how he got in.'

'The back door was open,' pointed out Jacob, accurately.

Nan shuddered and drew her purple-flecked cardigan more tightly round her bulging blouse. She still had a magnificent figure, despite her age.

'There you are!' she cried, in indignation. 'You let people live with you out of the goodness of your heart and they never think of taking care. Lights left on and doors left open! You'd better call the police, John. Not that I want *them* traipsing all over my front room—let alone what the neighbours will think—oh, I do wish Len was still alive!'

Nian shook away the confusion of two meanings at the end of this speech. Again, he understood both of them clearly: Nan's words had sounded *Oh, ei dohnt noh!* and she had not actually mentioned her husband Len out loud at all. But there was no time now to think about this.

'We'd better see if anything's been taken,' said Mr Rush, nervously. 'The police will want to know that.'

Oh *help*, thought Nian, yet again. What would

165

they find in the front room? What if they came face to face with a whole Tarhun squad?

He kept behind the others, ready to make a run for it, as Mr Rush shambled to the front room door.

Whatever happened, he wasn't going back.

Mr Rush opened the door a thumb's breadth and squinted through.

'Nothing here now,' he said, pushing the door open wide. 'It's all quiet.'

Nian was almost more surprised than relieved, because the Tarhun always, always, always hunted in packs.

But perhaps the Tarhun had come here by mistake. Yes, that must be it: the Lords had sent the Tarhun to hunt for him, and one of the great boobies had blundered into the passageway while he was poking about by the statue.

'I don't think anything's been taken,' Mr Rush went on, helplessly.

Nan shouldered her way past him and went round peering at the ornaments that littered every surface. Nearly all of them were over-coloured models, but on the mantelpiece was a chunk of glassy stone. Nian nudged Jacob.

'What is that stone?' he whispered. 'It looks like other world stone.'

'Dunno,' said Jacob. 'Grandad brought it back, I think. Nan! Where did that stone come from?'

'What, that? Bognor. Your grandad picked it up on the beach so he could weigh down his newspaper. It's not worth anything, but he took a fancy to it, somehow.

But then he never did have any taste.' She sniffed. 'And neither did this great oaf of a tramp. Couldn't tell quality when he saw it, I suppose,' she ended up, rather offended.

'Oh . . . er . . . right,' said Mr Rush. 'And . . . er . . . he just ran out, did he, when he saw you?'

'Well, he gave a jump. He looked frightened to death, to tell you the truth. Must have been simple. A lot of these tramps are. He just barged past me and bolted.' Nan wrinkled her nose in disgust. 'And he was absolutely filthy, too. Disgusting!'

Mr Rush tugged nervously at a lock of his greasy hair.

'It'll be quite stressful having the police round,' he ventured.

'Not half as stressful as knowing the great lout's loose on the streets. Where's that phone?'

Nian backed quietly towards the stairs. The further he got away from the front room the better, because if the passageway was still open someone else might come through at any minute. Nian made for Jacob's bedroom, but he'd only got as far as the landing when someone ran up the stairs after him.

Robyn was looking nearly as scary as Nan.

'I thought you said your blasted passageway between the worlds would be closed by now!' she said.

'Well . . . I thought it would be,' answered Nian, very worried. 'It *should* be.'

'You *thought*?' howled Robyn, her eyes as sharp as wasps.

A thumping heralded Jacob's arrival.

167

'Hey, keep your voice down, Rob,' he said. 'Nan's phoning.'

She turned on him, then.

'Keep my voice down?' she echoed, incredulously. 'We've got extra-terrestrial monks invading the house, and you tell me to *keep my voice down*?'

'I do not think he wished to invade,' explained Nian, apologetically. 'But he was not a monk: they're all weedy. It must have been one of the . . . one of the *Tarhun*,' he finished up, using the proper word for want of an English one.

'Oh, great,' said Robyn, scathingly. 'That's all right, then, isn't it? Brilliant. And what the *hell* is a Tarhun when it's at home?'

'They . . . they wait hand and foot on the monks,' said Nian. 'They go out and look for . . . for brilliant boys, and take them to the monks.'

'*Fantastic*,' snapped Robyn. 'Do you mean we've been invaded by a professional *kidnapper*?'

Nian nodded unhappily.

'Oh, hell's bells,' said Jacob, in wonder. 'And Nan's calling the police, as well. I mean, it's bad enough us harbouring an illegal immigrant, but as for helping to organize an actual invasion . . . '

'I did not wish this,' said Nian, unhappily.

Robyn frowned ferociously at a really nauseating picture of an extra-fluffy lynx-cub. Or something.

'The police might not come,' she said. 'They'll probably think Nan's round the twist. Nan doesn't want them here, anyway, because of the neighbours.'

168

'I did not wish your nan to be not fantastic,' said Nian, feeling guiltier than ever, but Jacob suddenly grinned.

'Actually, I think she's quite enjoying the excitement, in a bonkers sort of way,' he said. 'She seems perkier than she has been for ages. And she's going to phone her friend Mrs Hinde, next, to tell her all about it, and Mrs Hinde will probably invite Nan round for coffee so they can have a good moan and a nit-pick.'

'Oh well, everything's all right, then,' said Robyn, sourly. 'As long as Nan's happy, what does it matter if Dad is stressed so he can't work so we never ever ever have any money, and if the alien mafia's rampaging through the streets?'

But Jacob only grinned even more widely.

'Where do you suppose the Tarhun will go?' he asked. 'Do you think he'll go charging around accosting people and yelling *your money or your life*!'

Robyn shot him a perishing look.

'It's not funny.'

'Yes, it is,' said Jacob. 'Well, it is as long as he's not here, anyway.'

But Nian was still uneasy.

'The Tarhun will have the screaming abdabs,' he said. 'And he will have no English. This world is very difficult, with many very strange customs.'

Robyn sighed.

'Yeah, like not wearing your pyjamas all day,' she said. 'Put some proper clothes on, Nian. You can't do anything in those.'

169

|||| |||| |||| |||| ||||

Nian heaved his heavy body back up onto the top bunk to change back into the stupid shirt and ludicrous tie. Robyn sat hunched morosely below him, and Jacob draped himself over the windowsill. Nian was very glad everyone had stopped talking, for the effort of understanding, especially the double-speak of mind and tongue, was getting almost more than he could bear.

But that world never seemed to be properly quiet, even when everyone had finally stopped speaking. There was always noise: mechanical noises from the kitchen, or the wailing and thumping that Jacob had explained dismissively as *raydeeoh wun*. And now there was the continuous swooping noise of the beetle-wagon things. Nian didn't want even to try to imagine how they worked, but he was just getting to the point where he could ignore them, when the noise changed. One of the swoops grew an edge that mounted into a screech, and then into a tearing squeal that ended in a loud thumping *smack!*

'It's a crash!' exclaimed Jacob, in amazed delight. Nian hastily waggled his head out through the collar of the stupid shirt, but by that time Robyn had elbowed her way into the space at the window next to her brother and blocked Nian's view completely.

'*Wow!*' said Jacob, in tones of the most heartfelt and reverent satisfaction.

'What is it?' asked Nian.

'He's going to get away!' said Robyn.

'Oh, fantastic, he's knocked his helmet off! And look, here's another one coming!'

As Nian dived forward along the bed a new noise made itself heard—a wild whooping that swelled louder and louder. Nian looked out over Jacob's head. The road was littered with shiny hummocky beetle-wagons, all at strange angles. There were people, too, and several of them were running as fast as they could. Nian gasped, for now a yellow-and-blue-squared beetle-wagon was belting down the road towards them and screeching to a stop right in front of the house.

And now a voice was roaring out hoarsely above all the other noises:

'I'll have your guts for chitterlings, you effeminate clods of stinking dung-rat dinner!' it bellowed, and not in English, either, but in good plain Thian; and it was then that Nian realized he was watching the arrest of a member of the Tarhun by this world's police.

The Tarhun was unusually large and strong, even for one of his calling, and he was concentrating on bashing policemen's heads together. There were already two policemen sufficiently damaged to be sitting on the ground out of the way. one was talking to a small black box. All the way along across the road Nian could see excited faces peering round handfuls of grey curtain.

Then there was an awful circular howling like a troop of scalded swing-gibbons and another zooming wagon came into sight. It was larger and squarer than the others.

'Ambulance,' breathed Jacob, blissfully.

It screeched up and some doors at the back flew open. The men that jumped out didn't seem to be policemen, because instead of attacking the Tarhun, who was now whirling round in circles with a blue-clad figure clinging desperately to each arm, they ran to the most injured men and began to check them over for damaged bits. Nian wondered if he ought to go down and try to explain things, but he decided they were probably too excited to listen, particularly the Tarhun, who had shaken off one policeman and was trying to strangle the other one.

'Just *wait* till I tell them at school!' said Jacob, happily, as the thrown-off policeman staggered to his feet only to be floored by an ungainly but effective shuffling movement that Nian recognized as pure *Pirt-Pu*, which was the Tarhun form of unarmed combat.

The least damaged of the policemen was still talking into his black box. Nian wondered if it was some special way of making a will.

The Tarhun suddenly let out a blood-curdling roar, dropped the mostly strangled policeman, shook off the other one, who had launched himself bravely at the Tarhun's ankle, and turned and ran. And

172

Nian saw, with mingled terror and relief, that he was heading straight for the house.

'It might be good if he comes in,' he said, but very doubtfully. 'Then he can go back to his world.'

'You want us to let him in the house?' asked Robyn, incredulously. 'That homicidal lunatic?'

'Oh, good *grief*,' said Jacob. 'Look at Nan!'

All the other inhabitants of the road were still peering out worriedly from behind their curtains, but standing four-square by the garden gate was a short and indomitable figure in a violently purple tunic. The Tarhun was running full-tilt towards her, but Nan gave no sign of flinching. She stood, with her legs planted a foot apart and her arms folded. Nian couldn't see her face, but something in the way her blue hair quivered told him she would have given anybody pause.

She paused the Tarhun all right. He began to gallop slower and slower until he was very nearly running on the spot. Behind him two more yellow-and-blue wagons zoomed up. The policemen who jumped out had transparent shields and round shiny bonnets.

'*Riot police!*' murmured Jacob, in ecstasy.

The policemen advanced steadily with their shields linked together. The Tarhun looked over his shoulder at them, looked back at Nan, and galloped more slowly still.

Nan's shrill voice came up to them, even through the window.

'You ought to be ashamed of yourself!' she yelped. 'Galumphing about and terrorizing a respectable widowed woman!'

'*Go, Nan,*' murmured Jacob, awe-struck.

The Tarhun couldn't have understood a word Nan said, but all the fight suddenly went out of him. He came to a halt in front of her with his head hanging down and his great hands dangling loosely by his sides.

'Now you go along quietly!' cried Nan, irritably. 'Brawling on the street! I'll have you know this is private housing, and we don't have your sort round here!'

A policeman with stripes on his arm limped cautiously up to them.

'Mrs Letitia Rush?' he began. 'I take it this is the man you reported, madam. Can you—'

'Of course he is,' snapped Nan. 'How many long-haired hooligans do you think we get in this road? Go on, handcuff him, then, before he gets violent again!'

The sergeant, looking almost as cowed as the Tarhun, produced some metal rings linked with a chain and proceeded to clip the Tarhun's hands together with them. The Tarhun looked pathetic by then. Nian heard him say just one thing as he was ushered firmly away to one of the undamaged police wagons.

'Why won't you let me go back to my own world?' he asked plaintively. And then a policeman slammed the door on him.

The ambulance men were helping one of the policemen into their wagon, and the other policemen were retrieving their hats and examining the damage where one wagon had crashed into another.

'Looks like the show's over,' said Jacob, regretfully. 'Cor, Nan was terrific, though, wasn't she?'

'The excitement really seems to have done her good,' admitted Robyn, thoughtfully. 'I think she even looks more upright than usual.'

Nian cast a Thought at the figure by the gate. The inflammation inside Nan had died down a lot, and the loneliness had been replaced by seething outrage.

Nan had the last word.

'And in *my* day,' she shrieked after the retreating policemen, 'the police knew how to keep law and order!'

None of the policemen looked pleased.

﹋ ﹋ ﹋ ﹋ ﹋|

'You are the sort of person,' said Robyn, sourly, to her brother, as the police cars escorted the ambulance away, 'who would throw half a dozen eggs into the air and then remember he couldn't juggle.'

Jacob grinned. He'd gone all pink and extra-cheerful since he'd watched the arrest of the unfortunate Tarhun.

'Where will your police have taken him?' Nian asked.

'To the police station,' said Robyn. 'He'll be locked up facing charges: grievous bodily harm, resisting arrest, causing a breach of the peace, and goodness knows what else.'

Nian considered this. In all sorts of ways this almost certainly served the Tarhun right. But even so Nian couldn't help feeling a little uneasy.

'I should go and tell them about him,' he suggested. 'I could tell them he is not of this world, and frightened.'

'The Tarhun's just laid four policemen flat and been responsible for hundreds of pounds worth of damage to two police cars,' said Robyn. 'It wouldn't make any difference if he was the Grand Vizier of Kathmandu with sunstroke.'

Jacob's eyes glowed with the joy of it.

'I wonder what the Tarhun's telling them?' he said happily. 'Do policemen investigate mysterious passageways between worlds? If not, who does? MI6? Or is it all in *The Z-files*? Or do you think they'll just slap him in the loony bin?'

'He can't talk English,' pointed out Nian. 'He won't be telling them anything.'

Jacob gave a sudden hoot of laughter.

'They'll be sending all over for someone who can understand him!' he said, snorting. 'There'll be Swedes and Estonians and all sorts driving in to try to make him understand. And he won't be able to make a statement!'

'Yes he will,' Robyn pointed out. 'The Tarhun's from Nian's world. He'll be able to learn English straight away, like Nian did.'

Nian shook his head, relieved to be able to explain now he'd got the burning-at-the-stake thing sorted out.

'No. The Tarhun are like you. I can speak English only because I have powers.'

'Have you? Really?' said Jacob, fascinated. 'Cor! What sort of powers?'

'Powers . . . powers in my skull. When you speak I know what you think. That's how I know English. And I can . . . move in the air,' he went on, stumbling round the holes in his vocabulary. 'And I can tell what will be, a little. And make plants grow. And help people who are damaged.'

'Wow,' said Jacob, happily. 'You're a super-hero! *Fantastic!* Hey, just think of the things we could do. We could—'

But Robyn's face had sharpened into an expression of acute interest.

'What? Do you mean you can *cure* people? Is that just broken arms and legs, or can you do inside things? Because Dad'll never really talk about it, but he's been ill for years and years. It means he can't get a job, so we've always been really short of money.'

Nian felt the dizziness that accompanied this lie, which was not a lie. Dad *wasn't* ill—and perhaps he never had been—but he had allowed people to believe that he was, and that had been as strong as a lie.

'He will soon be well,' said Nian, without the words or will to explain any of this. 'I have used my powers on him.'

Robyn and Jacob gaped, and oh, it was a huge, an enormous satisfaction to have shut them up at last. Nian hadn't realized how *annoying* it had been to go from being the most powerful person in the world to being an ordinary insignificant boy, and he felt an irresistible urge to show off.

'Look,' he said, picking up a small pink canister from a shelf, and placing it in front of him on the rug. He concentrated on it as hard as he could. He strained and he strained . . . until the thing rocketed up like a flushed peak-grouse, hit the ceiling with a *thud*, burst off its lid, and fell again, discharging a cloud of heavily perfumed smoke all over everything.

'What the . . . ' gasped Jacob, and then he got a mouthful of foul-tasting dust, and choked.

'It's that revolting talcum powder Nan gave me,' cried Robyn, in dismay. 'Whatever did you do that . . . ' and then she sneezed violently four times.

Nian's eyes were full of tears. The fog of cheap perfume was truly stomach-heaving, so he grabbed blindly for the pink pot and fumbled it back upright.

In, he thought fiercely. *Smoke—in!*

It worked in an instant. The room went from an unbreathably dense and revolting pong to absolute clarity in a finger-snap, and when Nian had wiped away the tears in his eyes he saw that the smoke had formed a tall white funnel-shape which was swirling swiftly and gracefully back into the tin.

'That was not what I intended to happen,' said Nian, inadequately.

Jacob was wiping his lips on his sleeve to get the taste out of his mouth, but Robyn was glaring at Nian as if he'd turned into a mud-skunk.

'That was *incredible*,' Jacob said, hoarsely but reverently. 'Just like *tear gas*.'

Robyn found the tin top and pressed it firmly home.

'Has no one ever told you that your powers are dangerous?' she asked, and went and opened the window.

'Yeah,' said Jacob, in great excitement. 'With powers like that he could do anything. He could have his own TV series. Yeah, he could make a fortune on telly. Good grief, with powers like that he could take over the world!'

'No he couldn't,' snapped Robyn. 'Nian, you mustn't take any notice of Jacob. He is a complete and total—'

'No I'm—'

But then there was a howl, a long hair-raising howl, that mushroomed up through the floor and stopped them all in their tracks.

'What . . . ' began Jacob.

'That wasn't your nan,' said Nian, uncertainly.

'No,' said Robyn. 'That was Dad!' And they all threw themselves out of the room and elbowed and stumbled their way down the musty stairs. They got to the bottom just as the front room door was swinging open.

Dad was gazing straight ahead, but his eyes were glazy and unfocused.

Nan bustled through from the kitchen.

'What's happened *now*?' she demanded.

Dad groped blindly for the door frame.

'A hand . . . ' he gasped hoarsely. 'A withered hand, coming out of the wall! I . . . I . . . '

And he fainted.

꠸꠸꠸ ꠸꠸꠸ ꠸꠸꠸ ꠸꠸꠸ ꠸꠸꠸||

It took quite a long time to bring Dad round. Robyn and Jacob worked away frantically at undoing his buttons and chafing his hands, and Nan stood over them barking instructions and grumbling because she'd messed up her hair jumping out of the way when Dad had fallen over. She'd moved with surprising agility, though; and when Nian checked he found that the inflammation in her stomach was very much reduced.

Dad was inclined, once he woke up, to stay where he was and whimper, but his mother was having none of it.

'Well, what did you expect?' demanded Nan. 'I *told* you there were peculiar things happening in there. Think what a shock it was for *me*, at my age.'

Dad took a tremulous breath.

'It was terrible,' he said. 'I can manage to cope with . . . but this hand . . . it was all withered, as if it was dead. And it came out of the wall at me!'

Nian felt a new pang of alarm. *A withered hand*. Not one of the Tarhun, then: one of the Lords.

'Did it grab you?' asked Jacob, breathless between horror and delight.

'Well . . . it sort of groped about.'

Nan snorted.

'What *you* need, John, is some fresh air,' she said. 'So you can get my car out and give me a lift to Mrs Hinde's.'

'But what if something else happens?' asked Dad, feebly, ignoring Jacob's and Robyn's attempts to help him up.

'Well, *I* don't know, do I? But would you rather it happened while you were *in*? Now, I must go and see if I can sort out my hair. Blessed comings and goings. It's like living in Piccadilly Circus!'

Robyn and Jacob managed to coax Dad up and settle him down in the back room, but Robyn's face was grim as she filled the kettle to make Dad a soothing cup of herbal tea.

'What have you done to Dad?' she demanded of Nian. 'He's never fainted before. Has the stuff you've been doing to him made him worse?'

Nian wondered for an awful second if that might be true: these were other-world creatures, and they might react differently from ordinary people. But then he remembered Nan, and was reassured.

'No. My powers are good,' he said. 'I have made your nan better. You can see that.'

Robyn shot him a suspicious look.

'Nan wasn't ill,' she said, shortly.

Jacob ran a set of bony fingers through his hair.

'I don't know about that,' he said. 'She has been sort of quiet and grey and extra-whingeing just lately.'

'So it's thanks to Nian that she's gone bossy an grouchy, is it? That's really stupid!' (*Grayt!* was the

182

sound she made: but surely that word meant good, not stupid?)

Nian yet again thrust this puzzle aside and stood firm in front of Robyn's accusing glare.

'Your dad fainted because of the hand that came out of the wall,' he said. 'That was not my powers.'

Jacob thoughtfully tore a tea bag to pieces.

'I suppose that sort of thing might make *anyone* faint,' he said. 'And, hey, it'd be brilliant if Dad really was getting better.'

'Oh, yes, wonderful,' snapped Robyn. 'So now we've just got to worry about organizing somewhere for Nian to spend the night, being prosecuted for smuggling illegal immigrants, and the small fact that the house is still being invaded by a gang of violent kidnapping thugs.'

'That hand was not Tarhun,' said Nian, for what it was worth. 'The Tarhun are all fat. The hand must be of . . . of the men with powers.'

Robyn regarded him sourly.

'Oh, that was one of your monks, was it? One of the ones with the supernatural powers who could destroy us all in the blink of an eye. Well, that's total rubbish (*reeallee brillyunt*) then.' And she flounced off to take Dad his tea.

Jacob swept the tea leaves off the bench and emptied them into a plant pot that stood on the windowsill.

'Actually, I think you may be OK to stay here for one more night,' he said. 'Mum really likes you,

183

especially since I told her you wanted a job helping with the sheep. She's really keen on people getting jobs. But, the thing is, if people are coming here looking for you, then you'd really be better off leaving.'

He went into the hall and edged the front room door open a little way.

'There's nothing here now. Hey, perhaps the passageway is closing, and that's why your monk could only get his hand through.'

Robyn, coming back from taking Dad his tea, glared at him.

'And what if it isn't?' she demanded.

Jacob considered.

'We could brain anyone who comes through with the poker,' he suggested, indicating the magnificent brass twirly affair by the grate. 'People arrive quite slowly, so there'd be plenty of time.'

Robyn rolled her eyes in scorn.

'That's just so *moronic*!' she said. 'Don't you *get* it? There's a *whole world* behind that fireplace. We can't fight back a whole world!'

'But my world does not wish to come,' pointed out Nian. 'My world hates other worlds.'

'Then why do they keep pushing themselves through?' asked Jacob, reasonably.

'And why didn't that Tarhun turn round and go straight back home?' demanded Robyn.

Nian shrugged.

'I expect he was too frightened to think,' he said. 'Before, when one of the Tarhun came to another world, he went back very quick, though he left behind much . . . good quality things.'

'Good quality things?' echoed Robyn. 'What sort of things? Money? Gold?'

'Treasure!' exclaimed Jacob. 'Hey, is your House full of treasure?'

'Yes,' said Nian. 'Treasure. But no. Not now. Before was ages ago. The Tarhun was carrying treasure, and when he came to another world there was a gold man, or perhaps a boy, who held an old lamp in a . . . in a place under the . . . the big thing like that.' He pointed at the lump of transparent rock that sat on the mantelpiece.

'A cave!' said Jacob, in great excitement. 'And a boy with golden skin: someone oriental! Robyn, that must have been *Aladdin*! Was that the boy's name, Nian? Aladdin?'

'I do not know that.'

'I bet it was, though,' said Jacob, thrilled. 'Hey, I'm the new Aladdin. Just think, Robyn, I'm *legendary*. Cool!'

'Aladdin is just a pantomime, idiot,' said Robyn, dismissively.

'Doesn't mean it's not true,' said Jacob. 'For all we know all the pantomimes might be true.'

'Oh, yeah,' said Robyn, exasperated. 'We'll be queueing up behind tabbies in Shoemart, next. Oh good grief. Why did your blasted corridor have to come out *here*, Nian?'

That was a question that hadn't occurred to Nian before, but it was a very good one. This place didn't seem to be anywhere in particular. It was just an ordinary house, inhabited by an ordinary family (except that there was no such thing anywhere, in any world—the memory of his own family tore through him like an arrow: Mother, Father, Grandy, Miri, Tan: all so far, far away beyond the great black gulf of nothingness between the worlds).

The black gulf studded with diamonds, shining in the light of all the tiny suns.

'I think it is because of that stone,' said Nian, pointing. 'I think it once came from . . . from the mum world, and it has a . . . a wish to bring the worlds together.'

'Yes,' said Jacob. 'That would explain . . . quite a lot of stuff.'

'But that doesn't work,' said Robyn, impatiently. 'It might be sort of magnetic, but that doesn't explain how it got here in the first place.'

'When the worlds . . . when they move,' said Nian, frustrated, out of words and with his brain screaming to settle into easy Thian, and not speak this bumping barbaric English any more. How did you say *earthquake*? How did you convey the huge stirring of the rocks that Grandy could hear amidst the silence of the valleys, and the massive explosions that jolted and cracked them open in great steaming wounds? And how did you explain the first, biggest explosion of all, that had sent the rocks of the mother world out across the universe to end up even here, in Nan's front room?

But Nian didn't have to explain it. Because even as he was clenching his fists to try to drag the words from the air, the floor began to shiver under his feet.

|||| |||| |||| |||| |||| |||

The earthquake began with a long vibration, and then a jolt that caused all the little china figures to tremble their way a whole inch nearer the edges of their shelves and then waver heart-stoppingly before trembling back again. Dad howled again briefly, and Nan came to the top of the stairs calling out: 'It's all right, it's stopped!' And then she stomped down the stairs.

'Ridiculous,' she said, crossly, peering round at all her ornaments. 'We never had earthquakes when I was a girl. Still, it doesn't seem to have caused any damage, I suppose that's something. But it's one thing after another. I was putting on my lipstick, and I nearly rammed the thing right up my nose. Goodness knows what Mrs Hinde will say.' And then she went out to say it all again to Dad.

Jacob was fairly jumping with excitement.

'*Wow!*' he breathed. 'Isn't it all *fantastic*?'

Nian wasn't excited at all by the earthquake, because they happened all the time in his world. But he was alarmed by the news that they were rare here.

'I wonder what'll happen next?' Jacob asked, glowing with joy.

Robyn swung round accusingly to Nian.

'This is something else to do with you, isn't it?' she said, with dangerous intensity.

'I don't know,' Nian said, but he was increasingly uneasy. There was something about the earthquake that had changed this place. It wasn't a scent, or a sound, or anything he could see, but it was as if some part of his own world had reached out and tapped him on the shoulder. And Nian had a sudden, gut-wrenching conviction that something terrible was going to happen.

And then it did.

'*Nian!*' said a voice.

They all jumped and spun round towards the fireplace: but there was no one there.

'Who was *that*?' asked Jacob, and even he sounded a bit scared.

Nian knew the answer, but he could not bear to say his name in case it called him, made him somehow more real.

'*Nian*,' said the voice again. '*You must answer me.*'

They'd all taken a step backwards.

'It wants you,' said Jacob, though he could only understand the name. 'It's calling you.'

'Who is it?' asked Robyn, sharply.

Nian swallowed down a big expanding mass of fear.

'It's my teacher,' he said, blinking at the ugly fireplace and telling himself that Tarq was a whole world away.

'*I hear your voice*,' said Tarq, in the calm, careful

tones of the Lords of Truth. '*Nian, the worlds are beginning to tremble: so you must come home.*'

Nian felt another small quake vibrate through the soles of his shoes—but he told himself it was nothing.

'*I am home!*' he said, in his own language. '*This world is my home now!*'

When the voice came again it was fainter, and it crackled and spat.

'*That is not possible,*' it said. '*The worlds are tied by the passageway you have made, and it is time for them to move on. You and the Tarhun must come back so it can close, for the passageway is pulling both the worlds to pieces.*'

'What's he saying?' demanded Robyn. Nian turned a stricken face on her.

'He says we've got to go back—me and the Tarhun—or the passageway will make both our worlds fall apart!'

Jacob and Robyn looked at each other.

'It's probably a trick,' said Jacob, but he spoke doubtfully. 'He's saying that so he can capture you again.'

Another tremor vibrated through the floor. Nian tried to believe what Jacob was saying, but he knew in his heart that Tarq was telling the truth.

'No,' he said, miserably. 'Tarq wouldn't tell lies. Not like that. It's true. It's true. So . . . so I'll have to go back.'

'Oh *no*!' said Jacob. 'But you can't go back there! It's all spooky and horrible. And it's *wrong*.'

'But of course he's got to go back,' snapped Robyn.

'Either Nian goes back or we all die: all of us. All of us, in both the worlds. There's no point in that.'

Nian swallowed the large lump that had swollen in his throat, for this was the end, the end of hope, and the end of any life that might be called *his*. He'd have to go back and let himself be swallowed up, annihilated, by the power of the Lords.

'*My son!*' The voice was fainter still, just piercing through a mounting wave of crackling.

'*I don't want to come back*,' said Nian, though he knew it was all hopeless. '*Not to waste my life*.'

'*It would not be waste, for we have the mightiest of callings*,' said Tarq, almost gently. '*We deal in Truth*.'

'*No you don't*,' said Nian, furious and desperate and despairing. '*You trade in lies!*'

There was a pause. Then the voice came again, louder.

'*Tarhun!*' it called. '*Quickly! Carry the Lord Nian back! Be guided by my voice!*'

Nian almost launched himself back into his own world just for the pleasure of strangling Tarq.

'*The Tarhun isn't here*,' he almost shouted. '*He attacked people, like the fool he is, and now he is in prison!*'

'*But he must return!*' said Tarq, hastily. '*Already the fabric of the House is crumbling!*'

Good, thought Nian, and for a moment the destruction of the House seemed worth anything. But Robyn was saying something, and he had to steady himself so he could understand her.

'*How long till there's really serious damage?*'

Tarq's voice was so far away under the rustling of the tearing worlds that Nian could only just make out the answer to the translated question.

'Not long. A few hours, perhaps—I cannot tell. But no one else must use the passageway, or the whole world . . .'

But then a crackling hiss rose over his words and whatever he was going to say was lost.

A few hours: and Tarq wasn't even certain about that. That was enough to put a chill on Nian's anger.

And if it hadn't been, the next tremor was enough to sober anybody. Three china children toppled off the mantelpiece and crashed into pieces on the tiles below.

卌 卌 卌 卌 卌||||

Dad, wrapped in several coats, shuffled to the door of the front room.

'I'm driving Nan to Mrs Hinde's,' he said, bravely. 'And then I think I'll go down to the Health Food Shop. All this stress won't have done me any good, I'm afraid.'

'Dad,' said Jacob, 'we've got to go down to town. Can you give us a lift?'

'Well, Nan's in a hurry,' said Dad. 'But if you're ready . . . '

'We won't be a minute.'

Robyn started squawking and waving her arms about again as soon as the door closed behind Dad. She'd been doing that for ages, and Nian hadn't been even trying to understand her. He was trying to think. His last year had been dedicated to developing his powers, or trying to develop them, and now he was going to have to use them for something really vital.

'Town. Is that where the Tarhun is?' he asked, only remembering to use English at the last minute.

'Yeah, he'll be at the police station,' said Jacob.

Robyn clutched at her head in disbelief.

'But what are we going to *do*? Tell them that the only way to save the world is to let that violent loony go?'

'Course not,' said Jacob. 'They'd never believe that. No. We'll have to help him to escape.'

Robyn nearly took off, herself.

'And how are you going to do that?' she screeched. 'Knock out all the policemen with talcum powder bombs?'

'I don't think we've got enough talcum powder,' said Jacob, slightly regretfully. 'But anyway, we don't need them. When I went on that trip to the police station in Year Seven we went round the cells, and they've all got skylights. If Nian can fly, then he can go up on the roof and let a rope down to the Tarhun so he can escape.'

That was at least a blessedly straightforward plan. Nian nodded.

'That could be done,' he said.

'Of course it can't be done!' howled Robyn. 'They'll have alarms and CCTV!'

'Well, Nian will have to watch out for wires and cameras, won't he?'

Nian was thinking rapidly. He didn't know this world well enough to understand properly what was involved, but if Jacob was suggesting it, it couldn't be impossible. Could it?

'You are absolutely the stupidest, most lunatic . . . ' began Robyn, but at that point Nian stopped listening again. He wished Varn were with him, for Varn knew the ways of towns and cities. Varn would know a man who could be bribed to let the Tarhun go.

But Varn *wasn't* there.

'We'll need some rope,' said Nian. 'And your-world clothes for the Tarhun, for the way home.'

The clothes were easy. Jacob sneaked into Nan's bedroom and stole a peaked cap and a voluminous raincoat that had belonged to Grandad.

'He'll look like a dirty old man,' said Jacob, as he stuffed the raincoat into a bag. 'But that'll be a good thing if it makes people avoid him.'

Robyn still had Nan's scissors.

'They'll come in for the Tarhun's ponytail,' said Jacob, pleased. 'It's so long and bright yellow everyone's bound to notice it.'

'Just stop,' said Robyn. 'Both of you, stop. You're just blundering on, and we need to sort all this out sensibly. So. We have to rescue a mad alien from prison in order to save the world. Right.' She blinked several times, and then took a deep breath. 'OK,' she went on. 'I think I can cope as long as I don't let myself believe it's real. So. Where's this rope?'

Jacob rubbed his chin.

'That's a good point,' he admitted. 'I don't think we've actually got any.'

'But we must have,' said Robyn, showing signs of panic again. 'We must have a bit of rope somewhere.'

'OK. You go and get it, then.'

Robyn walked round in two tight circles, glowering. 'Isn't there something we could use instead?'

'In my world,' suggested Nian, 'I have sometimes climbed . . . er . . . things that grow round trees.'

194

'Oh, yeah,' snapped Robyn. 'And have you got one on you, Tarzan?'

The front door slammed on the sound of Nan's nagging voice.

'We've got to go,' said Jacob, making for the door.

'But there's no use—'

'I know,' said Jacob. 'But Nan won't let Dad wait!'

As he spoke there was a particularly violent tremor that sent them clutching at the walls, and from outside a throat-clearing noise that broke into a low *vrooming*. Jacob grabbed Nian's sleeve and ran. They burst through the front door as Dad's wagon was reversing out of the drive. Nian couldn't help but be a bit relieved to see that Dad's wagon went fairly slowly—but then he supposed it was a cheap one. Robyn tugged open a door in one side of the wagon and squirmed her way along the leather seat. Jacob bundled Nian in after her, jumped in himself, and slammed the door.

The wagon was only just wide enough to take them. It smelt of nauseatingly harsh things that Nian had never smelt before, and the leather of the seats was oddly sticky.

In the front Nan was grumbling about layabouts, ghosts, and earthquakes, and blaming it all on a lack of parental control. Nian tried not to be alarmed by the fact that apparently it was essential to tie themselves to their seats with heavy straps. It seemed unnecessary when the wagon hardly moved faster than an ox. But Nian soon discovered that the wagon went a lot quicker forwards. It went stupidly fast: it swerved round corners so that everyone got squeezed against each other. Nian got dizzy with the way everything whizzed backwards past them, and the fact that the oxen pulling the wagon were just, incredibly, *not there* made him feel as if someone had whizzed his brain into mush.

Dad pulled the car to a jerking stop outside a dingy house, and came round to escort Nan up the garden path. She had a brave, suffering look about her. Nian felt a fresh pang of guilt.

'I am sorry I did grisly things to your nan,' he said.

'Oh, don't worry,' said Jacob. 'She always *was* incredibly grisly. And she really seems to be thriving on it.'

'She was ill, before,' said Nian.

'And here's Dad,' said Robyn. 'Though *he's* still pottering along like a pensioner. Are you *sure* he's better, Nian?'

Nian cast an enquiring Thought at Dad as he came up to the car. Dad's whole being, mind and body, was slack with disuse, but there was nothing actually wrong.

'He is quite well now,' he replied.

'That's great,' said Jacob. 'So, just a pity about the world-falling-to-bits thing. This hasn't really been brilliant timing.'

'I'll tell you something,' said Robyn, grimly, 'if we *do* survive, then Dad's going down the Job Centre first thing on Monday.'

Dad eased himself into his seat and pulled at the strap that hung looped from one wall of the wagon. Nian looked at it thoughtfully. It looked strong—strong enough to hold even a very fat member of the Tarhun—and it was probably long enough. Nian nudged Jacob.

'That is like rope,' he said in a whisper, pointing at the strap beside Nan's empty seat.

Jacob followed his eyes and winced.

'Yeah,' he said. 'But Nan'll go berserk when she finds out: it's her car, and everything to do with it costs a fortune. Robyn!'

'What?'

'Shh! *Have you got the scissors?*'

'*What for?*'

Jacob pointed at Nan's strap and made snipping motions with his fingers. Robyn's blue eyes nearly bulged right out of her head.

'*Nan'll kill you!*' she hissed. '*And it's against the law!*'

Dad negotiated their way between two parked wagons and a man sitting between two wheels and progressing apparently by magic. Nian hastily looked away: this world was much too much for him.

'*But we need it,*' whispered Jacob.

The wagon swerved suddenly left round a white hummock someone had left in the road.

'*Just don't expect me to take the blame, that's all,*' hissed Robyn, as the wagon came to a stomach-lurching stop because an old lady and two boys with fishing nets were walking across in front of them.

Robyn handed Jacob the scissors. She had her fingers crossed, which was a warding-off-evil sign in Nian's own world, too. Jacob bent down to the floor of the car and began sawing away at the belt. Luckily, Dad was fully occupied avoiding all the wagons that were whizzing around, all seemingly intent on smashing into them.

The trees and gardens had mostly been replaced by grey stuff, now, and the road was lined with huge square buildings with ugly windows. The only greenery consisted of silly patches of grass like doormats, and dusty toffee-apple shaped trees.

By the time Jacob had finished sawing laboriously through both ends of the strap, Dad was driving the wagon up and down a grey square which was full of rows of other wagons. Nian shifted in his seat, because there was so much tension and worry in that place that it made his nose tingle. Jacob had only just got the seat belt rolled up and stowed away in his bag when Dad turned into a space between two other wagons. Nian felt relief diffusing through everybody as Dad pulled a lever that shuddered the wagon into quietness.

'Now,' said Dad, as they got out. 'You'll make your own way back, won't you, because I think I ought to have my biorhythms analysed while I'm here, and then I've got to see about my aura. Have you got enough money for the bus?'

Under their feet the earth shook again, quite gently, but with a prolonged shudder.

'We'll manage,' said Jacob, quickly.

'I'll see you later, then.'

'I thought you said Dad was better,' said Robyn, as they left Dad scooping jingling coins from his pocket.

'He is,' said Nian. 'But he does not know.'

'Oh,' said Jacob, frowning. 'But then . . .'

'Easy,' said Robyn, darkly. 'We'll tell him. Right. OK. I am calm and in control, and none of this is real. So. Let's go and find the police station.'

Nian followed them. The busy swooping of the wagons beside the path was confusing, so he kept his eyes fixed firmly on Jacob's back. After a few minutes Robyn turned aside from the main road and into a quiet lane between tall grey barns.

Here there were no wagons at all. Nian trudged along through bits of blowing rubbish. His legs were still tired from his walk yesterday, and, apart from that, it was his bedtime. He felt oddly isolated, as if he were in a bubble, cut off from everything around him. And he had so much to do. When he got to the police station he had to rescue the Tarhun, and after that (if they succeeded) they had to get back to Jacob and Robyn's house.

And then he had to go back to the House.

That would be the end, then: the last thing he'd ever do.

'How far is it?' he asked, and he was surprised by how feeble his voice sounded.

Jacob stopped immediately.

'Sorry,' he said. 'I keep forgetting you've been shut up for ages. We'll take a rest.'

'We haven't time,' said Robyn, impatiently.

Jacob shook his head.

'But there's no use hurrying if Nian hasn't the strength to use his powers when he gets there, is there? And look at him, Rob. He's pretty much worn out.'

Nian wanted to say something to stop them arguing but he was too grey-feeling to work out how to do it.

'Sorry,' he whispered, and let his knees buckle until he was sitting on the ground.

'But this is no good,' said Robyn, restlessly, walking up and down. 'He can't just sit there, the whole world's going to blow up! *Two* whole worlds. Oh good grief, this is *completely* ridiculous!'

'I know. But if we push him—' Jacob broke off suddenly. 'That's it!'

'What?'

'Wait here,' said Jacob, and ran off across the road and out of sight round a corner.

Robyn stared after him for a minute, and then she began prowling up and down again. She did give Nian a tablet to eat, though. It was very sweet and chewy, and actually rather comforting. It was only a minute or two before Jacob charged back round the corner pushing a large wire box on wheels.

Robyn's jaw dropped.

'A supermarket trolley,' she said, accusingly. 'Jacob, you delinquent. Where did you get that from?'

'The Co-op. Come on, help me get Nian in. There's no time to lose.'

200

That was almost the first time in his life that Nian had been glad he was small. The trolley was exceedingly teeth-rattling and uncomfortable, but it was worth it for the chance to rest. Only one person tried to stop them, a stout woman with scarlet lips who screamed at them: 'That's for food, that is! Not your dirty bum!' but Jacob swerved round her and ran on.

'Sorry,' said Robyn, perfunctorily. 'It's just that we're saving the world at the moment, and so we're in rather a hurry.'

Jacob brought the trolley to a halt behind a tree, and helped Nian out. They were outside a high brick building with a flat roof. There seemed to be a walled yard at the back.

'The cells are in that block there,' said Jacob, pointing. 'You'll have to walk along the roof and look down the skylights until you find the Tarhun. If you fly up from here you won't have to go inside the yard.'

He handed Nian the bag that contained the strap and the disguise.

'Good luck,' he said. 'Er . . . good luck. You'll be brilliant.'

Nian sat down on the cold stone of the path and called up his powers. He tried his hardest to despise the earth; but that was more difficult than ever, especially now he could feel, faintly but unmistakably, the trembling underneath him that heralded its destruction.

Concentrate! he told himself savagely. I *hate* this stupid world that covers me in disgusting fumes. I *hate* these stupid people, who don't understand how easy their lives are. I *hate*—

And then there was a rush of air around him and he had the sickening sensation of having left his stomach on the ground. He threw himself forward onto the palm-stinging gravel of the roof.

Nian bit off a cry of anguish. He got up cautiously, tenderly brushing the grit from his hands. Jacob had been right about the skylights: there was a whole row of them stretching along the roof. So many prisoners. He wondered what their crimes could have been.

He walked softly over the roof to peer into the first cell.

Nian stopped a careful distance from the edge of the roof and peered back down at Robyn and Jacob. They looked squat from above. Jacob was leaning against the wall in a way that would have drawn growls from Father.

From Father, whom Nian would never ever see again.

'That was quick,' said Jacob, squinting up. 'Have you found him?'

'The Tarhun is not there,' said Nian.

'*What?*'

'Are you sure?' asked Robyn, sharply, shielding her eyes.

Nian wished he knew how to say *I could hardly miss someone that size.* He was still lamentably short of usable English insults.

'I've looked in every cell,' was all he said. 'There is no Tarhun.'

They gazed at one another in dismay.

'But what can we do now?' asked Jacob. 'We've *got* to get him back. And we saw him arrested, so he *must* be here. Mustn't he?'

'He was handcuffed,' said Robyn, 'so he couldn't have escaped. Unless . . . Nian, is the Tarhun really strong?'

'Yeah,' said Jacob. 'Perhaps he's a sort of Superman. Nian, could he rip up iron bars with his bare hands?'

Nian's mind was zapped with a picture of a hugely muscly man flying through the air at great speed. He looked immensely noble, in a dumb kind of way, and he was wearing women's stockings.

'No,' he replied, dismissing this bizarre image as best he could. 'I told you. The Tarhun is ordinary.'

'Well, he *must* be here, then,' said Robyn.

'We'll have to go in and talk to the police, I suppose,' said Jacob. 'Tell them how vitally important it all is . . . '

'Yeah,' said Robyn, with scorn. 'And how long do you think it'd be before they sent for the men in white coats? One sentence or two? Nian, you'd better come down off that roof before someone spots you.'

'But then what *can* we do?' asked Jacob. 'Because, whatever it is, we've got to do it *now*.'

Nian looked down doubtfully. He could fly upwards all right, but so far coming down had always taken care of itself. The ground looked a long way away, but it was only really about twelve spans or so. Less than twice his own height.

The longer he thought about it the worse it would get.

He took a deep breath and jumped.

He only had a fraction of a second to absorb the hideous fact that things fell faster in this world. His feet thudded into the ground so hard that his legs folded and pitched him forward. He put out his hands to save himself, but he was moving so much faster than usual that they weren't strong enough.

His forehead hit the pavement with a quite appallingly hollow knock.

####### ⊬⊬⊬ ⊬⊬⊬ ⊬⊬⊬ ⊬⊬⊬ ⊬⊬⊬ ⊬⊬⊬

It hurt so much that for a second Nian hoped he was going to pass out. Jacob and Robyn were gabbling away in English, and hands were taking hold of his elbows to help him up, but his head was ringing so sonorously that it was as much as he could do to work out which way up was, let alone what they were saying.

And now there was a new voice, a deep man's voice, blaring above him. Nian swallowed down the salty taste from his cut lip and squinted up. Against the blindingly bright sky there was a large figure in a dark blue tunic and leggings, and a ridiculously flat hat.

Policeman.

Nian wondered vaguely about running away, but his head was too full of graunching, brain-bruising rocks to make any sort of movement reliable.

'Are you all right, sonny?' asked the policeman, with his hands on his nicely-creased knees. He was tall and burly and really extremely smart. His hair was combed back smoothly at the sides (how did these people's hair *stay*? Glue?) and he smelt sweetly of rotting herbs. But he was being kind, in a dreary way that made it plain it was his duty, and that personally he thought they were a pain.

'I hope so,' said Robyn.

'His head hit the pavement really hard,' Jacob told the policeman, wincing.

'Yes, nasty bump, that was,' said the policeman, in a very slight attempt at concealing his utter indifference. 'You'll have to watch where you're going, sonny.'

'Nian, *are* you all right?' asked Jacob, anxiously. 'Can you stand up by yourself?'

Nian had a go. The air around him was full of mauve floating blobs, but at least the pavement seemed to have settled back down on the ground.

The policeman seemed to decide he'd been nice enough.

'Well, clear off,' he ordered, though behind that meaning was a double-speak echo of his actual words (*yood betta bee mooving along*). 'You shouldn't be hanging around here, you know, this is the police station. You get a lot of fast cars about. Know how to cross the road, do you?'

Jacob blushed and nodded, and the policeman looked very slightly gratified. Jacob put out a hand to help Nian, but Robyn didn't budge.

'The police station?' she said, with a wild but determined look in her bright blue eyes. 'Good, this is the right place, then. This is Nian, and someone he knows was arrested this morning. Do you know anything about it? There was a fight in George Street.'

A curious expression compounded of stern disapproval and unholy relish came over the policeman's face.

'Ah yes,' he said, eyeing Nian with new interest. 'Yes, I understand they had a rare old time bringing him in. And now they can't find anyone to understand him. First they sent for an atlas, and then they sent for a globe, and then they tried Language Line, but all the bloke will do is cry out *Revaco Sabili Lasvate!* or some such, and tear at his hair.'

The policeman's accent was barbarous, and he'd mangled the words considerably, but Nian could guess what it meant: *may the Lords of Truth save me.*

'Nian can understand him,' said Robyn.

The policeman looked surprised.

'Really? Because we've never known Language Line defeated before. We were really beginning to wonder if the bloke can talk at all, or whether he was just making noises. Mind you, they couldn't get him to talk into the phone properly: he seemed terrified of the thing.'

A phone seemed to be a device on a string that let you hear the voices of invisible people. And they wondered that the Tarhun gibbered with fear?

'I can speak his language well,' Nian said.

'Hm. Well, I suppose in that case you'd better come with me. The Inspector'll certainly be glad to see you, and if you can just confirm what language he's speaking, then they'll be able to get on.'

Nian and Jacob and Robyn followed the policeman's broad back round the building, through a glass door, and into a beige corridor lined with chairs and bored people. Jacob looked scared, and Robyn particularly truculent, so Nian knew they were in great danger.

The policeman pressed a pattern of buttons on the wall that caused a lock to click open in the door beside it. He herded them through and down a shiny scruffy corridor. Large men kept coming out of doors carrying sheets of paper or grimy mugs. Nian wondered what all these men did when they were not catching members of the Tarhun. And he wondered exactly what it was that Jacob was so scared of.

The large policeman knocked perfunctorily at a door and ushered them into a dingy room that was mostly filled with a table. There was also a pretty autumn-haired lady in uniform, an amiable man in a hairy tunic, and a dark-eyed man with a case on his lap containing a whole heap of sheets of hartskin, and what appeared to be a triangular glass bread-case. They all looked up, and the amiable man smiled so nicely that for a moment Nian forgot to be afraid.

The Tarhun was there, too, but Nian noticed him last because he was slumped over the table with his ponytailed head on his arms.

'What's this?' asked the amiable man. 'Didn't know we were doing guided tours today, Douggie.'

From the way the policeman smiled, the amiable man must be very important indeed.

'They speak his language,' he explained, with a jerk of his head at the Tarhun. 'I found them outside,' he went on, with a smirk at his own cleverness, 'so, knowing as how you were in difficulties, I thought I'd better bring them in.'

'Thank goodness,' said the pretty lady. 'We were just wondering about going over to the Jewish old people's home to find someone who speaks Yiddish.'

The amiable man laughed ruefully.

'We've already had Mike in to try his Polish, and Maria to speak Italian to him, and *I've* tried him on the pen of his aunt and recited a few irregular verbs at him in German—but all he does is sit there with his head in his hands and jabber and rock. And he's completely terrified of the telephone, even when it's on the speaker system. Yasmin's even tried him with half the languages of the sub-continent, but it wasn't any good. And Language Line can't make head nor tail of him.'

He swung round in his seat to smile at Robyn. 'Come on, then, love,' he said encouragingly. 'You try and see if you can get through to him. If you'd just tell him we aren't going to hurt him, and that we need to ask him a few questions.'

'He needs to have his rights read to him,' said the dark-eyed man. 'And we ought to start recording.'

'Yes, yes, of course we should. Abbie, are we all right with the apparatus? All right, then. And we'll certainly let him know his rights just as soon as we've established communication, Mr Cohen. Now, love.'

'Er . . . ' said Robyn, and then blurted out the only word of Nian's language she knew. 'Tarhun!' she said.

The effect on the Tarhun was startling. He sat bolt upright, gazed wildly at Robyn, raised his handcuffed wrists supplicatingly, and then burst into tears.

'Well, we'll,' remarked the amiable man, mildly gratified. The pretty lady pulled a flimsy piece of white stuff out of a box and held it out to Robyn.

'You give it to him, love,' she said.

Robyn approached the huge sobbing man warily. She was right to be wary: as soon as she was within range the Tarhun fell to his knees, leaned his head against her, and carried on sobbing brokenly down her tunic.

'Nian!' she said, through a mouthful of grimy hair. '*Do* something!'

'Er . . . ' said Nian, because it was a long time since anyone had wanted him to do anything. Anyway, he'd no idea what to do. He could only think of ordering the Tarhun to attack all the police people and then make a run for it, but he wasn't sure about letting the Tarhun hit the pretty lady, and on the whole he rather liked the others. Nian pulled himself together and did his best to be lordly and commanding.

'*You must release that young lady*,' he said firmly, in Thian. '*I am a pupil of the Lords of Truth, and she comes under my protection.*'

The effect on the Tarhun was even more startling. He let go of Robyn as if she were red hot, leapt to his feet, and bowed very low over his handcuffed wrists. Then, just to make Nian feel completely and utterly ridiculous, the Tarhun got down again and prostrated himself along the shiny floor at Nian's feet. The dark-eyed man had to jump up out of the way to make room for him, and dropped the glass bread-case in the process.

It bounced.

'Bless my soul,' said the amiable man, fascinated, peering down over the table at the Tarhun's huge backside. 'Is he a friend of yours?'

'Not exactly,' said Robyn. 'But my friend Nian here's a . . . a sort of prince in their country, and they do things like that there all the time. It's quite primitive. And sort of a bit feudal.'

'He's a serf,' said Jacob, helpfully.

'Well, well,' said the amiable man, rather pleased. 'Well, there are never two days the same in this job, are there. Spice of life. But would you ask him to get up now and take his seat again, please, because

211

Mr Cohen has come in to be his legal representative, and we don't want to waste his time.'

'*Get up*,' ordered Nian. '*We are going to escape from this place and go back to our own world.*'

The Tarhun froze. Then he looked up at Nian with a wistful gleam in his piggy eyes.

'*Shall I wring their necks, Lord?*' he asked hopefully.

Nian wasn't at all sure what they were going to do.

'*Hold yourself ready to obey my orders. And sit down!*'

A bell rang sharply on the desk. The Tarhun panicked, leapt up again, and seemed about to try hurling himself through the barred window, but when Nian said his name he recollected himself and sat down again rather sheepishly.

The pretty lady picked a bone-shaped thing off a box.

'Hello? Yes, he's here, but he's interviewing somebody at the—oh. Oh I see. Yes. Straight away. Here he is.'

The amiable man sighed, and took the bone-shaped thing from her.

'Mulready here. Oh, hello, Brian, what can I do for you? What? Really? Oh, *Lord*! Anyone hurt? Well, that's a miracle. Yes, yes, right away. Of course. Priority alpha, all available personnel. That's all right. I'll be with you in fifteen minutes.'

He put down the bone-shaped thing and stood up.

'My apologies, ladies and gentlemen,' he said, 'but one of these earth-tremors has opened up a nasty crack across the motorway, so we'll have to put this on hold for a while.'

'Good heavens,' said Mr Cohen, gathering up his blue and white scarf and shutting his case.

'Abbie,' went on Mulready, 'will you get through to the radio and television traffic report people? No casualties, but it's the whole motorway, north *and* southbound, north of junction seven. You know the sort of thing: long delays, extreme caution, and avoid the area if possible. Got that?'

'Yes sir,' said the pretty lady, and made for the door.

'And I'd better be getting up there myself. I'm sorry to have brought you down here for nothing, Mr Cohen, but I'm sure you understand. Someone will be in touch again very shortly, naturally, and at least we'll be able to get a translation service set up in the meantime. Abbie, will you see Mr Cohen through security as you go. Thanks.'

He was shrugging on a flappy coat as he spoke.

'Douggie, you'd better take down these young people's names and addresses. And would you ring Norma for me and tell her I'm going to be held up. And we'd better get our friend here back to his cell. Make sure he knows he's safe, and that we'll have a proper fair inquiry into what's been going on soon. This young gentleman will help you make him understand. And make sure he's had something to eat and drink. Thanks.'

Mulready paused in the doorway.

'He still seems a bit nervous, so perhaps you'd better get some help to escort him back down to the cells.'

213

Douggie grunted, and eased the stout stick that hung in a holster at his side. The Tarhun looked hopefully at Nian, but Nian shook his head. He was alarmed by the reports of the crack in the motorway, but the Tarhun was going to have to escape quietly: they couldn't hope to get him home if they were chased.

'I'll leave it to you, then,' said Mulready. 'Thanks for coming in, kids, it's much appreciated. See you later, Douggie,' and he went out.

And this was the moment when there was a chance, just this moment, while Douggie was moving over to the speaking bone to call for help.

'Talk to the policeman,' Nian murmured to Jacob and Robyn. Then he turned to the Tarhun. '*Hold out your wrists,*' he said, carefully casual, '*I'm going to break the chain of your bonds, but the man must not see.*'

'Er . . . how much money do you earn?' said Jacob, randomly, and then bent over double as Robyn elbowed him in the ribs.

The Tarhun swung round a little so his back was to Douggie. Nian concentrated his powers on the middle link in the chain. The easiest thing would have been to melt it, but Nian was afraid he might burn the Tarhun in the process. He tried to twist the link so it snapped.

'Yes, I'd love to be out of here safely (*in the poleess*),' Robyn was saying, while Jacob's eyes bulged with the strain of trying to get his breath back. 'Er . . . navy blue must be terrible for showing up the bits, though (*mei fayvorit culler*).'

214

'Well,' said Douggie, ponderously. 'Suppose you're a good girl and help me explain to Tarhun here that he's got to go back down to the cells for a while, then. And tell him he can have a cup of tea while he waits, all right?'

Nian was concentrating too hard to speak, but Robyn gulped, and said 'Wogga magga velleeter mongy wuna!'

The Tarhun, taking this for English, ignored her.

'Oh dear,' said Jacob. 'I don't think he seems very well. Mucker wucker vranky?'

'I'd better call someone to assist,' said Douggie, picking up the bone-shaped thing.

The links in the chain were buckling nicely now.

'No,' said Nian, hastily. 'Er . . . not now.'

'Why not?'

Jacob seemed to be able only to open and close his mouth soundlessly, but Robyn blurted out:

'Because . . . because we're in a hurry. The world's about to end. (*Owr pairents will bee wundering wair wee ar*). Could you take our names and addresses down now, so we can be on our way? We can easily make something up so you can't trace us. (*Weed bee evva so graytfull.*)'

Douggie sighed a heavy sigh to show how much this was putting him out, put down the bone-shaped thing again, laboriously unbuttoned a pocket, laboriously took out a notebook, laboriously turned the pages, and drearily intoned, 'Name?'

The handcuff chain was on the point of breaking. Another few seconds would do it. Nian ignored Robyn's echoing double-talk as best he could.

'Robyn (*Emily*) Rush (*Brocklebridge*),' said Robyn, promptly. '22, (*56*) . . . ' She rattled off an address and then waited for the pencil to catch up. 'And this is my brother (*kuzzin*) Jacob (*Nicolas*) Rush (*Ponsonby*). What number is it you live at, Jake (*Nick*)?'

'Oh . . . er . . . twenty-two,' answered Jacob, weakly.

'Oh yes, of course it is,' said Robyn innocently. '22, George Street (*Mankroft Rohd*). And Nian here—'

The link snapped at last. The Tarhun looked up at Nian for orders.

'*Pretend to faint*,' murmured Nian. '*Then, when he leans over you, hit him.*'

'—is Nian, N-I-A-N, and he's staying at—'

The Tarhun gave a huge whooping groan. Then he half got up, clutched at his heart dramatically, rolled his eyes, went *aaaargh!* and keeled over in a clatter of chairs.

'What the—' muttered Douggie, and took two quick steps forward to investigate.

The Tarhun caught Douggie right on the point of his large jaw. The Tarhun hit him so hard that Douggie was actually knocked upright by the force of it. He stood for a moment with an astonished look on his face. Then he raised a gentle hand to caress his chin—before gradually and gracefully crumpling into a peaceful heap on the floor.

ЖЖ ЖЖ ЖЖ ЖЖ ЖЖ ЖЖ ||

'*Wow!*' said Jacob, awe-struck. 'What a *punch*!'

The Tarhun grinned bashfully and rubbed his knuckles with tender care.

A new tremor came. It vibrated the floor and died away, but it reminded them how perilously urgent everything was. Jacob began to pull the squashed raincoat out of his bag, and Robyn snatched out the scissors.

'*We must escape to our own world,*' said Nian to the Tarhun. '*The girl will cut your hair, and then you must put on these garments.*'

Robyn surveyed the Tarhun once he was disguised.

'I've never ever seen *anyone* so dodgy-looking,' she said.

Jacob looked at him, too, with a sort of dreadful fascination.

'Well, at least people will avoid us,' he said. 'Which way do we get out? Through the window?'

'We can't. It's barred,' said Robyn.

'Yes,' said Nian. 'And if we are seen it must not be known we are escaping. We must go back the way we came. And we must look happy.'

'Oh, yeah,' said Jacob. 'Nan's going to tear me limb from limb for taking that seat belt, I'm just assisting someone in an escape from custody, and the only thing that might save me is the fact that the world's falling to bits. Of course I'm going to look happy. How else should I feel?'

The Tarhun tied Douggie up with the seat belt, and found a handkerchief in Douggie's pocket that made an admirable gag. Robyn put the four different tapes that had been recording the interview in her pocket, tore out the sheet of notebook with their false names and addresses on, and then, in order to confuse everybody still further, tore another sheet out, wrote something on it, then tore it into the tiniest possible fragments and threw them in the bin.

'What did you write?' asked Jacob, putting a large yellow wad of hartskin under Douggie's peaceful head as a pillow.

'I don't know,' said Robyn. 'It was in code. Come on.'

The corridor was deserted.

'*Look happy*,' Nian ordered the Tarhun, whose face had settled into its accustomed Tarhun scowl. The Tarhun hesitated, then he lifted the corners of his mouth into an imbecile grimace that reminded Nian of nothing so much as the time he and Tan had fed the hog fermented apples. Nian opened his mouth—and then gave up. He hadn't the time or energy to make the Tarhun look normal.

The trouble on the motorway seemed to have taken

most of the policemen out of the station. There was what Jacob called a security lock on the first door they came to, but that was no problem: Nian melted it with one quick burst of Wisdom. They only saw one person in uniform, and he was the man on the counter, who was listening to a detailed description of a bird called a budgie from a man in a cloth cap very like the Tarhun's. The queue was even longer now, and so thoroughly bored that it was indifferent even to the vibrations of the earth tremors. Nobody bothered to look at the three agitated children and the surly man who made their way out through the glass door.

'Right,' said Jacob, as they took their first breaths of free air. 'How do we get home?'

'Quickly,' answered Nian. 'We do not know how long it will be before the worlds break up. What is the quickest way?'

'Taxi,' said Robyn. 'I think I've got enough money.'

'Just as long as we can be far far away from here before Douggie wakes up,' said Jacob, leading the way round the building. 'Nian, I think you'd better get back in the shopping trolley, because I've got an irresistible urge to run screaming all the way to the taxi rank.'

The Tarhun pushed the trolley: he seemed to think it an honour, and he was so strong he wasn't even annoyed by the fact that its wheels kept turning at right angles to the way he wanted to go.

'Why couldn't you have stolen a decent trolley?' snapped Robyn, as the trolley scraped her ankle for the second time.

Jacob shrugged.

'It must be something in-built,' he said. 'I think I must be the chosen-one as far as disabled trolleys are—oh *hell!*'

The last exclamation was wrung from him by the sight of the main street. The first remarkable thing was that there were wagons packed solidly end to end, not moving at all, and the other remarkable thing was that there was a three-span crack right across the road. Two of the wagons had wheels wedged in the crack, and they were all so obviously unable to move in any direction that many of the drivers had begun to study large sheets of hartskin, or had gone to sleep.

'Oh, hell's bells,' said Jacob. 'Whatever do we do now? There's no point in getting a taxi—nothing can get out of here with the traffic like this. And I bet they're diverting the motorway traffic this way, too, and making things even worse.'

'We must go fast,' said Nian, wearily, for he'd been jolted about so much in that trolley that he felt as if he was falling to pieces. 'The Tarhun can push me.'

Jacob and Robyn exchanged unhappy glances.

'I suppose we'll have to,' said Jacob, reluctantly. 'But it'll take us half an hour, at least.'

'If we've got half an hour,' said Robyn, grimly, and broke into a jog. Nian gripped the sides of the trolley and gritted his teeth to stop them banging together. But people had evacuated the buildings, and the crowd made it almost impossible to get the trolley along.

'This is hopeless,' said Robyn, when it had taken them two precious minutes to manoeuvre their way fifty paces. 'Could the Tarhun carry you?'

'I shall try to run,' said Nian, but even the effort of heaving himself out of the trolley was almost too much. He got out and staggered; he might even have fallen if there had been room in the crowd. A man in an apron put out a hand to steady him.

'You all right?' he asked.

Nian opened his mouth, but Robyn's tongue was faster.

'No,' she said. 'He's exhausted and not well (*ohvadyoo for hiz treetmunt*). We've got to get him home soon or goodness knows what'll happen!'

Robyn was a dangerous person, but she had good brains. Those of the crowd who heard made way for them, and the message was passed along. Nian was so tired by now that he did feel actually sick with weakness. He stumbled on as fast as he could, but he must have looked terrible, for people were staring at him in pity and alarm.

Once they got to the edge of the town the crowd thinned, but the wagons were still jammed end to end along the road.

'I wonder where Dad is in all this lot?' said Jacob.

'Having his aura touched up,' said Robyn, sarcastically.

They crossed a wide road and turned along it, but the sight of the long grey path stretching away in front of him made something inside Nian collapse.

His knees collapsed at the same time, and deposited him on the hard ground.

'But you can't rest now!' exclaimed Robyn.

'What's the matter, Nian?' asked Jacob, anxiously.

Nian stared at the path. He felt grey all through, somehow, to match it, but the Tarhun didn't bother with questions: he heaved Nian up onto his back like a sack and carried on running. Nian put his head down onto the Tarhun's hefty shoulder and tried to blank everything out.

'Is there anything I can do that will help?' asked Jacob, scarlet-faced, running beside him.

'I'm only tired,' said Nian. 'I was a farmer, once. I could work all day in the fields. But now . . . '

'You're more important than a farmer,' said Jacob. 'You're going to save the world. Both our worlds.'

Nian closed his eyes.

'If we're in time,' he whispered.

A period of bumping blackness followed. Nian was half asleep, but he kept catching tinges of colour that were Jacob's agitation, and Robyn's stitch in her side, and the Tarhun's impatience at their slowness. Then there came a time when Nian awoke properly to discover that riding on a Tarhun's back was the most uncomfortable method of travel in any of the worlds. They were in a quiet road lined with houses, and there was no traffic here at all.

'Is it very far?' he asked Jacob, who was jogging along all gangling and crimson and dogged.

Jacob was too tired even to look up.

'We're all right,' he said shortly. 'Try to go back to sleep.' Nian looked at Robyn. She was heavier than Jacob, not made for running, and he could sense the pain in her side.

This is all my fault, he thought.

He buried his head in the Tarhun's raincoat and closed his eyes.

Nian was roused from another period of blankness by the sound of a wagon woozing up behind them. It clicked to a halt, and a familiar voice said:

'Hi! Er . . . is something happening?'

Nian wearily turned his head. Dad was leaning over the passenger seat to peer up at them.

'Oh, Dad,' gasped Robyn, fumbling at the door catch. 'Thank goodness. Nian collapsed in town, and we've been carrying him all the way back. We've got to get him home.'

'Oh. Right. Yeah. So where does he live?' asked Dad, as the Tarhun lowered Nian to the ground. 'And . . . er . . . who's this?'

Robyn had a fast mouth and a quick brain.

'He's from Nian's country,' she said. 'And we need to get Nian to our house. That's where the passageway to his world is (*heez left hiz stuff*).'

'Oh. Well, in that case I can't see how I can get out of giving you all a lift, then (*doo let mee giv yoo a lift, er . . .*).'

'Tarhun,' said Jacob and Robyn together. 'But he doesn't speak English,' added Robyn.

'Tarhun.' Dad waved his hand in a come-on-in

223

gesture. The Tarhun hesitated, but Nian spoke to him and he climbed massively in.

'How did you get out of town?' asked Robyn, slamming the door. 'The traffic's solid.'

'Oh, the Health Food Shop was closed because they were short-staffed, so I drove up to High Green. Hey, Robyn, pass me Tarhun's seat belt, will you, and I'll do it up for him.'

There was a second's silence.

'We've got to hurry,' said Robyn, 'There's not time for a blasted inquisition, now. (*Eim wurrid abowt Neeun*).'

'Yes,' replied Dad, 'but you know what Nan's like about us obeying the law when we're in her car.'

Another second's silence, then:

'I can't. The seat belt's not there.'

Dad poked his head round so he could see the anchorage point, and then he went quite white.

'Jacob,' he said, completely aghast, 'what happened to the seat belt?'

Jacob swallowed.

'Um . . . I cut it off,' he said.

'But why did you do that?' asked Dad, in horror.

'Well . . . I really needed it.'

'But what for?' said Dad, his appalled eyes staring back at them from the little mirror that hung from the roof of the car.

'To tie up a policeman,' said Jacob, with a gulp.

There was a shaken pause, and then Dad started the engine.

224

'The really important thing is to get Nian home,' he said. 'But I truly hope, Jacob, that you have some very very good answers for when you come to explain all this to Nan.'

The rest of the journey passed in silence.

‖‖ ‖‖ ‖‖ ‖‖ ‖‖
‖‖ |||

Mum must have been looking out for them. She met them at the door. She looked tremendously pink and excited, and not tired at all.

'Come on in,' she called. 'Nan's back. And she's got something to tell us.'

Nian was feeling better for the rest the journey had given him. He shook his head when the Tarhun went to help him out.

Nan was in the hall, very upright, standing with her back to the front room door.

'Yes,' she snapped. 'Come along, come along, let's get this over with.'

The Tarhun, out on the drive, ducked down behind the car at the sound of her voice. He crawled round the back of it on his hands and knees, and then dashed crouching to the wall beside the porch. He stood there, out of sight, and swaying from foot to foot like a worried bear.

Nan was very brisk and very businesslike.

'I've made a decision,' she announced. 'I know it'll be an inconvenience to you, but there it is. I've decided that I don't want us to live together any more.'

Jacob and Robyn gasped. Dad, shaken, blinked at her.

'But we've always lived together,' he said. 'This is . . . this is our home.'

'You're telling me,' said Nan, grimly. 'And I've had never a moment's peace ever since you came back from your travelling that you said you had to do to find yourself. Hah! As if there was ever any trouble *finding* you. The problem was always tripping over you! Right from when you were a baby you would never sit nicely, but you'd always be lolling about on the carpet. And I don't know where you got *that* from, because it wasn't from your father, rest him, or me. Well, I've decided that enough's enough.'

'But where shall we go?' asked Dad, wrinkle-browed and pathetic.

Nan snorted.

'Oh, you always *were* useless!' she said. 'Flopping about making yourself giddy with your navel-gazing! But you don't really think I'm going to stay here, do you, by myself, in a haunted house with withered hands and ghosts looming here, there, and everywhere? No, John. I'm going to put *myself* first, for once. I'm going to move in with Mrs Hinde. She's got that great big house all to herself, and she's terrified of burglars, and you should have seen her with the earthquakes: I had to be quite firm with her. So anyway, I'm moving. I know you'll miss having a permanent unpaid babysitter and maid-of-all-work around the house, but my mind's made up. I've phoned the removal van—not that I'll take much, only my ornaments and personal things and the best tea set—and they're coming Tuesday. So if you'll excuse me, I'd better go and start packing.'

She walked with dignity across the hall and up the stairs. As soon as she was out of sight all the family began to jump up and down and punch the air in silent jubilation.

'I can have Nan's room, can't I?' whispered Robyn. Mum laughed, and Nian hungrily tried to catch her happiness. He tried to see into the future, to see them all living happily in this world that was so unlike his own, though just as rich and full and fragile.

Soon, very soon, he must go back to the House: go back, and have his life wrenched from him. But he wanted to live his own life so fervently that he could hardly bear it.

'Oh, John,' said Mum, softly. 'Isn't it wonderful? It'll be a struggle to pay for everything, but we'll manage. Oh, if only you were properly well then I'd have nothing else to wish for.'

A faint tremor shook the floor, and Nian had to go. He *had* to go, but there were things to be said, first.

'Mr Rush *is* well,' he said. 'I have made him well. He is healed.'

Mum smiled, rather tearfully, but shook her head.

'That's a really lovely thought, Nian,' she told him.

'And it's true, too,' said Robyn. 'Tell them, Nian.'

'I . . . I have powers for healing,' answered Nian, getting stuck with his English for the first time for ages. 'Mr Rush will tell you he is not ill.'

Dad looked shifty.

'Well . . . I suppose I'm not feeling too bad at the moment,' he admitted. 'And I haven't been hearing any . . . but that's just lucky, of course,' he went on, hurriedly. 'I'm afraid there's never going to be any long-term change. After all, we've tried everything: regression, and crystals, and all the therapies. I mean, the doctors have long since given up on me. This is something that I'm just going to have to do my best to live with, I'm afraid.'

'But it's not!' exclaimed Robyn, passionately urgent. 'Nian's *cured you*. He's made you better. Really he has. He can do all sorts of stuff like that.'

'Yes,' said Jacob. 'He cured Nan, too. Think how much better she is. She'd got quite feeble and quiet, hadn't she, but now she's really awkward and aggressive. Nian did that.'

Mum looked from Dad to Nian wonderingly.

'But surely . . . I mean, it's a lovely idea . . . '

She trailed off, full of doubt. But she had to believe it, otherwise Dad would be able to carry on backsliding and complaining and drifting and wasting his time. And Nian couldn't bear to think of anyone's life being wasted; not now, especially, when his own was about to be snatched away from him.

He took a step back and spoke to the Tarhun.

'*The old woman has gone, and it is time for you to return to the House,*' he said. '*Come inside.*'

The Tarhun sidled in slowly, sheepishly, his head down so that his cap hid his fat face.

Nian turned his English back on again.

229

'I came here from another world, and now I must return,' he said, and only he knew how bravely he said it. In his own language people talked of being *heart-torn*, and that was how he felt, as if someone was slowly but remorselessly ripping his heart into two. 'The Tarhun is from my world, too,' he went on, 'and it is we, by being here, who are causing the earthquakes. I am sorry, but I did not know it would happen.'

Mum and Dad were looking uncomfortable.

'It's just a game,' said Mum, tentatively. 'Isn't it, Jacob?'

'No,' said Jacob.

'*Take off your coat and hat*,' instructed Nian.

The sight of the Tarhun in his uniform rather frightened Mum—but it was nothing to the way it frightened Dad.

'It's the maniac who went berserk in the street this morning!' he exclaimed in horror. 'Quick, everyone, into the bathroom!'

'*What?*' said Robyn. 'But why?'

'So we can lock ourselves in!'

'He will not go berserk now,' said Nian. 'He wishes only to go home. Mr Rush, Mrs Rush, come and watch the Tarhun return. Come, Tarhun.'

The Tarhun darted a quick defensive glance round with his piggy eyes and then shuffled after Nian into the front room. Mum and Dad and Robyn and Jacob followed them.

As it happened there was hardly room for them, because a huge block of stone was taking up most of the rug. But no sooner had they seen it, and exclaimed, and run their hands incredulously over the licheny discs that crusted the surface, than it began growing miraculously soft under their fingers. It turned to the consistency of cheese, then pillows, then dough, and then it was fading until in a few moments it had disappeared again completely.

'But look,' said Mum, bewildered, 'whatever . . . '

'That was the statue from the garden in Nian's world,' Jacob told them. 'I've been there. I've sat on it. It's on top of a mountain, in a monastery with a wall all round it.'

Nian had just a little time left here. Just a little, a little, and he would not waste it. He breathed in the free air of this busy world.

'*Walk towards the fireplace,*' he ordered the Tarhun. '*I shall follow you when I have made my farewells.*'

The Tarhun went down on one knee and made the deep salute of his class.

'*Farewell, and soon meeting, Lord,*' he said. Then he stood up and bowed to the others, turned towards the fireplace, took two steady paces forward—and faded impossibly to nothing.

Dad muttered something rude and jumped behind Mum. Robyn rolled her eyes.

'There's no need to look so poleaxed,' she told him, witheringly. 'Nian told you it was going to happen.'

'But . . . where's he gone?' asked Dad, in terror.

'Back to his own world. To Nian's world. Where he should be.'

Dad sat down very suddenly on a velvet chair.

'I'm not sure I can cope with this,' he said. 'Sue! I think I might be going to have a turn.'

'No you're not,' said Robyn, swiftly, as Mum patted his hand. 'You're not going to have any more turns. Don't you understand? *Nian's made you well.* You'll be able to get a job!'

Dad turned even paler, then.

'I'm not sure—'

'Yes,' said Jacob, triumphantly. 'And you said the Health Food Shop was short-staffed. They might take you on there.'

'And then we'd have *money*,' said Robyn, her blue eyes sparkling like glaciers. 'Money, and my own room! I'm going to paint it imperial purple, and have cacti all along the windowsill.'

Even Mum was looking thoughtful.

'You'd be quite good at the Health Food Shop,' she said. 'You'd be able to discuss people's ailments. You've always enjoyed that.'

Dad's eyes had taken on a wary and highly mulish look, but the earth was shuddering again under their feet.

'I must follow the Tarhun,' said Nian, sadly.

Jacob sighed.

'Yeah,' he said. 'You'd better come up and get your clothes.'

When they came down again Dad was still flapping about like a beached flop-fish.

'But look, hang on, this is all very well,' he was

232

saying, harassed. 'But what was all that about tying up a policeman? You're not telling me that was true, as well?'

'Of course it was,' said Robyn.

'Yes,' said Nian. 'Of course it was true. Jacob only says things that are true.'

And as he spoke he found he properly understood the echoing double-talk that had been disturbing him ever since he had arrived. He had been understanding English by listening to people's minds, and Jacob was the only one whose lips always said what his mind thought.

More liars, more lies: was every world full of them?

But there was no time to wonder about it now. There would never be time to think about it.

'The seat belt was needed to free the Tarhun from prison,' he went on.

Dad ran his hands feverishly through the limp chaos of his hair.

'But look,' said Mum, alarmed. 'That means Jacob and Robyn are in really serious trouble. And the police won't be interested in stories about other worlds.'

'No, it's all right,' said Robyn, still glittering with triumph. 'I gave them false names and addresses. And anyway, it was the Tarhun who did all the assaulting and tying up. So if they *do* trace us, we can just say we were frightened when the Tarhun attacked Douggie—the policeman was called Douggie—and so we ran away. And we can blame anything else on Nian. So there shouldn't be any problem.'

Mum looked from one to the other of her children and sighed.

'I suppose this does explain all the peculiar apparitions and ghosts and things,' she admitted. 'Poor old Nan.'

'Nan's been given a new lease of life,' pointed out Robyn. 'She'll be able to moan about us all day. She'll love it. And I shall have a *room of my own.*'

'And so shall I,' said Jacob. 'Peace at last.'

Nian was glad for them, but the end of his life was rushing closer and closer like a tunnel's mouth. In just a few minutes perhaps even the memory of this would be wiped away.

There was no point in waiting.

'Go in happiness,' he said.

Mum caught hold of him and gave him a hug such as he hadn't felt for a year, and would never feel again. He leant his head against her and told himself that the worlds were worth his life.

'Are there people waiting for you where you're going?' Mum asked.

It was easier not to explain.

'Yes, there are people.'

'And will you be able to come back here?'

He shook his head at that, suddenly unable to speak.

'It works a bit like cogs,' explained Jacob. 'There're loads of worlds all turning each other. Aren't there, Nian?'

Robyn's blue eyes sparked with interest.

'But in that case you can still travel, even if two worlds have turned away from each other,' she pointed out. 'You could go from world to world until you got to whichever one you wanted. Couldn't you?'

Nian was so struck with this that he had to stop to work it out. Robyn might be right: you couldn't join two worlds with a passageway for more than a few days, but there was no obvious reason why you couldn't keep moving on and on. Which meant . . . might mean . . .

A sudden new tremor sent them reaching for the walls. There was no chance to think, no point in hoping.

'I cannot stay,' said Nian, again. 'Goodbye.'

'You'd better take Grandad's Bognor rock with you,' said Robyn.

'No, don't do that,' said Jacob. 'If you do that there'll be no connection between the worlds any more. And all the *Wherevers* will go away.'

Dad twitched as if he'd backed into a pitchfork.

'The *Wherevers*?' he said. 'But . . . does this mean the . . . the . . . do you mean they're actually *real*?'

'Course,' said Jacob.

Robyn looked suspiciously from one to the other— and gave up.

'I think a bit of normality will do you good,' she said. 'Take it, Nian.'

The rock was cold: colder than anything in that room should have been. Cold as a mountain-top, and as pitilessly hard as the will of the Lords.

Nian took a deep breath of the warm air. He felt as if he were on the edge of a cliff, and if he did not step over the edge now then he was not sure he'd ever have the courage to do so.

'Live well,' he said.

And then he took two steps towards the fireplace. And fell.

He went down, down, into nothing, and the darkness swept over him. He opened his mouth to scream, but there was no air to hold the sound. He grew cold, and colder, but now there were thousands of speckles of white around him, and the tiny sharp disc of a faintly mildewed moon. He unclasped his hands and the stone of the mother-world shot from his grasp in a dazzle of brilliance and away he knew not where.

And now here were a thousand fleeting visions: blue seas, and golden walls, and green waterfalls, and something else—something shooting upwards to hit his feet and send him stumbling to a standstill beside a square statue, and leave him gasping and gasping for air in the faintly rosy dimness of the beginnings of another world's dawn.

And the torpor and lifelessness of the House of the Lords of Truth surrounded him, and crept closer with every breath.

$$\cancel{||||} \cancel{||||} \cancel{||||} \cancel{||||} \cancel{||||}$$
$$\cancel{||||} ||||$$

'My son,' said a soft voice behind Nian.

Nian spun round.

Tarq.

Tarq seemed even smaller and more frail after the large people of Jacob's world.

Nian had seen many faces during the last day—more than he had seen in all the rest of his life—and he found himself looking at the old man with new eyes. And it was almost as if Tarq were blind. Tarq could stand here in the garden and not even see the arching brambles because their beauty was far beyond the little steps he had made towards the Truth.

And Nian pitied Tarq, because even the most carefully planned of Tarq's explorations was as nothing compared with the beauty of the garden.

Nian gave one last look around at the garden, at the sky: but he could see more than that. He could see further. He could see the mountains, rising out of the mists that lay cradled in the valleys.

For the House was gone—at least, Nian thought so for a moment. Then, when he'd gasped and looked again, he saw that it was only part of the House that had fallen. A wide arc had been tumbled into rubble, and so had part of the Outer House beyond that, so that now Nian was looking down into the vivid fields that shouldered their way up through the mists to the ice-veined mountains.

Varn would be there, somewhere, making his way home. And Nian's family was there, too, working and playing and resting.

Nian made a fierce, brave effort, and was glad for them.

'There have been severe earthquakes,' explained Tarq, quietly.

Nian was glad of that, too. Indeed, he was savagely, triumphantly happy that he'd damaged the House, and that Varn, at least, was free.

And I am alive, he thought: but it was an empty triumph, for soon he would be gone.

'Come into the House, my son,' said Tarq.

The garden door stood ajar. The dawn sent a flush of pink along a strip of the floor, but beyond that slant of light everything was dim and shrivellingly dry.

'This is a bad place,' said Nian, loudly, against the curdled clouds of power that hung ready to smother the life out of him.

Tarq regarded him with his pale, mad, blinkered eyes.

'This is the House of Truth,' he said. 'Come.'

And Nian stepped over the threshold.

Nian felt the eyes at once: sharp eyes in dark corners.

Were those Bran's? Or Grodan's?

They were the eyes of the Lords, and what did it matter which one?

A thought-dart flew invisibly at him and stabbed into his mind; he winced, and faltered.

'This way,' said Tarq, calm as a frozen pond.

But there, over there: more eyes.

And here was another dart of thought, of what they called Wisdom, what they so falsely called Truth. This one lodged painfully inside Nian's brain. Nian shook his head fiercely, like a bull stung by an oxfly. The dart came away, but it was barbed. It tore his flesh as it came loose, leaving a smarting, distracting wound, and the misty swathes of the power of the House oozed into it. Nian stumbled briefly, but walked on.

Another pair of eyes.

Nian flinched away from what was coming, so that this time the dart glanced off his skin without taking a proper hold. It burst on the wall beside him in an invisible flash.

Something inside Nian glowed for a second: a small surge of satisfaction.

I am alive, he thought, again. *And Varn is, too.*

The next pair of eyes had a reptilian shine to them. That must be Rago, then. Nian watched closely for the thought-dart he was going to launch.

Rago was crafty: he aimed his dart wide, to bounce at Nian off a carving round a doorway. But Nian was young, and his reactions were fast, and he was lighter in this world than he had been in Jacob's. He knocked the dart away with a wild swipe of his hand, and found himself grinning with heart-thumping fear, but with a sort of triumph, too.

Beside him, Tarq's quiet footsteps faltered a little.

They had come to the Council Chamber of the House of Truth, now. Nian passed through the doorway and to his wonder found himself not under white stone vaulting, but under the wider arch of the sky. The jigsaw of stones that made up the roof had been shaken apart, and now the chamber was covered in shimmering silken blue.

But the idiot Lords would soon cast a wall of Wisdom (Wisdom? No!) to keep out rain and suns and starlight.

Behind him, a muted flutter of soft-soled shoes was sounding along the corridor. The Lords were following, one by one, all thin and dry and ignorant. Nian looked into their faces as they came through the doorway. They were like moles, that shuffled along their burrows and thought that worms were sunlarks.

And here was a heron-like youth. Nian looked at Caul, mild and vague, and Nian found that he was angry. Caul was young. He should be full of life, of vigour, not creeping along like this with blinkered eyes.

Now all the Lords were here: a dozen of them. And they were nothing more than a shambling, suspicious, ignorant assemblage in aid of nothing. Nian opened his mouth to tell them so, but now there was someone else in the doorway. Someone taller and broader than any of the others.

And it was Varn.

Varn.

'My son Nian,' said Tarq, softly. 'Your mind is much disordered. Let us soothe away your cares and worries.'

But Nian was looking at Varn, and he could have cried at the pity of this other wasted life.

'I thought you were safe,' he said, despairing, and Varn looked at him with eyes too dark to fathom.

'It was a close thing,' he said, softly. And with the words he hurled a phalanx of bitter thought-darts at his friend.

Nian ducked instinctively. Most of the darts burst on the wall behind him, but one seared an acrid trail along his cheek.

Nian gulped back a sob at the completeness of this betrayal; even as he did he knew that it was not really Varn who had attacked him. Varn was dead and gone, for these mild old men, these Lords, had destroyed Varn as surely as if they'd torn out his heart.

And at that knowledge Nian discovered again that he was angry. He'd been angry when he'd first arrived in the House, but then he'd not understood his powers so well—and since then he'd been obliged to contain his temper. But now he could be angry: now he could be *furious*.

Nian gathered together his powers.

'Beware, Lords,' said Grodan the Healer, in a cold and velvet voice. 'The boy thinks false thoughts.'

'Attack!' said Rago, harshly.

Three more darts of Wisdom zipped through the air. Nian threw up a hand and absorbed the power of the first, and ducked the second, but the third dazzled him. It burned swiftly through the bones of his forehead and his mind was flailing, crashing about with blinding light and tumultuous voices.

I SEE YOU I SEE YOU I SEE YOU I SEE YOU I SEE YOU!

The sheer force of it swept away every other thought, nearly collapsed him to his knees.

I SEE YOU I SEE YOU I SEE-SEE-SEE-SEE-SEE . . .

No! he screamed, though he seemed not to be making any noise. *Let me alone! Let me alone! GO!*

Silence.

Nian took a huge gasp of relief, and then another. The air had grown very sweet, like corpseflowers, although there was a sour edge of fear and anger in his mind that clashed with the honey-sweetness to make a scouring taste like the tearwort that Grandy dosed them with when they had colds . . .

Grandy?

There was something important about Grandy. Or was it some other old lady he was almost thinking of, who was possessed of her own sharp sourness?

But that was a trivial outside thing beyond the . . .

Beyond the.

Beyond the what?

Mountains. Yes, mountains.

242

Yes. Green glassy mountains iced with snow in winter.

Far and

Long

Away ago, that was, though.

But still . . . but still . . . but still *real*.

'His mind is still unruly,' said someone, close.

And at that Nian clutched at his anger again. He stood up straight and let it scorch away the honey-calm the Lords had tried to drown him in.

It left his mind absolutely crystal-clear.

He looked round him at the Lords, who were killing him, and he stepped back against the cold white wall, at bay. Most of the Lords were old men, older even than a few minutes ago, much older, for those darts of Wisdom were eating up their powers.

But Nian was strong, yes, and he would go down fighting.

Another dart. Nian swiped it contemptuously aside.

And here was another, from Caul. Nian could see the frowning effort it cost, though it was a puny thing that was nearly spent before it reached him. He let it fizzle out harmlessly against his sleeve.

But here was another. Grodan had edged round and sent it skidding along the wall. Nian saw it at the last moment, dodged too late, and got caught on the elbow.

The dart's power had sizzled to nothing long before it reached Nian's mind, but it stung like a tiger-bee. Nian reacted instinctively: a flare of brightness left his hand and zapped Grodan in the face. Grodan made a sound like a shocked frog and crashed back against the wall.

There was a moment of complete silence. Grodan put up a shaky hand to his temple, then he collapsed gracefully to the floor, and lay still.

'The boy is recalcitrant,' spat Rago. 'Vicious.'

'We must work together,' said Bran.

'But how?' asked Firn.

Then Varn spoke.

'This is the House of Truth,' he said. 'And Truth must be our weapon.'

Nian stood and faced them all: but he was afraid, because though the men facing him were small and thin and weak, now their eyes were glowing.

'Yes,' said Tarq, softly and almost sadly. 'We will discover the Truth of Nian.'

Nian braced every sinew of mind and body to resist more darts of Thought, but instead something else was forming in the eyes of the Lords: undulating ribbons of darkness were coming towards him, rippling strongly, like eels. Nian swiped out at them, made a double, a triple mind-wall. He conjured up a whirling knife—but the black ribbons came on at him, slippery and inevitable.

And now they had reached him. They were piercing his skin. They were burrowing into him like filaments of ice, wriggling into arms and legs and chest. Nian clutched at them, trying to catch their black tails, but they slid slimily through his fingers.

244

And now his body was being slivered into segments. The ice-worms were infiltrating him, making their way like hungry gut-lice into every secret, particular part. And as they went his flesh was shrivelled and desiccated in the flat white cold.

Nian knew he was perishing, was dying in that disinfectant waste. He made a great effort and called on everything he had ever been taught to fight them, but as soon as his powers met the ice-worms their cold flared brighter, brighter, slicing pain into his eyes and lungs and every part of him.

He must have lost consciousness for a moment—a blink of blackness that buckled his knees and found him staring past his fingers at the white flags of the floor—and then he was rolling onto his back to the toppling edge of the steps that led down to the Council Circle. And now he was bumping and wincing and crashing every one of his bones in turn on the jutting flagstones of the steps.

He ended up on his face. Every one of his nerve-ends was screaming, throbbing, contracting, connecting, short-circuiting in swift blazes of agony. It hurt so much he gave up. He flung away all his strength, all his powers, in one desperate attempt to end everything at once.

His powers burst out of him and Nian was left in a huddle on the stone floor.

He lay, waiting, and he was himself, just himself.

The pain would soon be gone, now, for the worms were spreading their icy darkness through his veins, and soon all that would be left was . . .

245

Truth?

Oh no. No. The Lords spoke of Truth, but the Truth did not require this violence or destruction, for the Truth lay in heaps, in profusion all around them. The Truth did not halt things, freeze them, wither them, as the Lords' powers did; nor would it turn aside a storm or lift up a tile against the force that held it down on the earth from which it had sprung. The powers of these Lords, these thin, mild, arrogant men, were for death, sterility. For anti-truth.

'Does the boy still live?'

'He breathes.'

'Is he tamed, though?'

'He must be, surely. His powers have never been well-controlled. He could not have fought off such an attack.'

No, Nian could not have fought off this attack: not if it meant using powers like those the Lords were using. Nian could never have let such blackness, such evil, take hold of him.

Never. Not though he had been strong himself, once, and full of the will to live.

He remembered the green valleys, and the mountains, and the glory of the suns that rose above them. Oh, and here was the power of Truth, that took its strength from the turning of the mighty worlds, when all the Lords did was struggle ignorantly against it.

Nian remembered the worlds as he had seen them, fine and shining, and as he did they seemed to spin towards him, closer, and closer, until their clear light bathed him.

Yes, he thought, appreciatively. This is how it is.

He lay in the light of the turning worlds, and each of them was full, brimming over, with Truth. And he opened his arms, so that the light fell upon him, over him, through him.

And as he did, the black worms that had tunnelled into him disintegrated. They softened, first into slime, and then into vapour. And all the parts of himself that had been pierced, laid open to the merciless view of the Lords, began to join together again, and Nian felt a first new spark of warmth—his own, and Grandy's, the world's suns', and even of the single sun of Jacob's world.

He lay, healing, as the power of the million worlds dissolved the lies, and destruction, and sterility that had had him in their grip.

Nian pushed himself to his knees. Now that he had seen the Lord's powers as they truly were, and had thrust them completely away, he could feel the power of the turning worlds expanding through him. It swept through him until he was strong, stronger than the white walls of the House itself.

He got easily to his feet and looked round at these greedy little men, who were using their puny powers to clip the wings of this extraordinary world.

And the anger that had been simmering inside him for a year began to boil. He might have brought the roof crashing down on them all if the roof had still been there. He reached out his hands, that were strong with the power of the worlds, and he grasped the mists of Wisdom that curdled smotheringly through the air. He tore them asunder and with a flick of his hand he destroyed them utterly.

|||| |||| |||| |||| ||||
|||| ||||

There was a blinding flash of light, and a breeze gusted through the room. The air was instantly clearer, and Nian could sense the freshness that told him he was on top of a high mountain.

'Nian?' said a voice: Varn's voice. 'But . . . but what are you doing here? I thought you'd escaped to your new world.'

But Nian's mind was following the breeze as it rushed outwards from the Council Chamber and around the hollow circle of the House of Lies. It went swiftly, scouring each pale corridor of a millennium of carefully piled lies and deception. It swerved round the curve of the walls, bounced over rubble, met itself again, and spilled back into the Council Chamber in an invisible spurt of joyousness and freedom.

Nian laughed in amazement and triumph.

All the Lords were blinking round, now, bewildered. Caul put a thin hand to his temple.

'But . . . my powers are less,' he said, uncertainly. 'Much less. They have shrunk so that . . . so that I can no longer see the paths of Truth.'

'Good!' said Nian. And laughed again.

'Tarq!' snapped Rago, the eldest and most shrivelled of the Lords. 'What will happen if a storm comes? How will we stop the snows?'

'I do not know,' said Tarq.

'You can't,' said Nian, still gasping with the shock and joy of what had happened. 'But it doesn't matter: not once you've mended the roof, anyway. You can go sledging!'

Rago snarled, but a smile came over the face of Grodan, who was only about fifty years old, though as bowed and scrawny as a summit vulture.

'I used to go sledging, as a boy,' he said. 'It was like flying. The snow used to sparkle where the suns caught it.'

'Yes,' said Bran, beside him. 'And in the winter, when the snow cut us off from all the world, we would sit round the fire and eat sausage. My grandmother used to tell us stories.'

Firn's eyes blinked.

'Sausage,' he said, wistfully. 'Sausage and pancakes.'

Astoundingly, Grodan began to look quite animated.

'On pancake days my mother used to save some for us to take to work next day,' he said. 'She spread them with honey and rolled them up, and you had to save water from your flask to wash your hands because they got so sticky.'

Caul was looking around him as though seeing the place for the first time.

'I used to go to school,' he said. 'I liked to study, so

my parents thought I might make a schoolmaster. I was at school when the Tarhun discovered me and took me away.'

All the Lords spoke now. They all had tales of the outside world of their boyhood, before the Tarhun came: tales that had been forgotten for ten years, or twenty, or fifty.

'And in *my* day,' Rago snarled, at last, 'boys had respect for their elders! We wouldn't have dreamed of going about wrecking things like this. We wouldn't have dared!'

And at once the Lords' eyes fell on Nian again.

'And this is not just mischief, a boy's defiance,' said Firn. 'He has destroyed the mists of Wisdom, a thousand years of Thought. Our powers are reduced almost to nothing.'

But Varn stepped forward, and he was the tallest of them all.

'*My* powers are not reduced,' he said, and boosted himself up high above their heads to stand on one of the ledges that had supported the roof.

The Lords shuffled backwards, peering uneasily up at him.

Varn picked up a tile that was still balanced on the top of the wall. He took aim with it at the old men below him.

'Shall I?' he called down to Nian.

Nian called to mind the future: the hurtling tile, the gashed head, the fall, the blood, the endless cooped-up fear and enmity.

'No,' he said.

'But—'

'No,' he said again, more firmly, and somehow his voice echoed louder in that roofless chamber than was quite possible. Varn glanced at him, and then he jumped down to take his place by Nian's side.

The Lords peered at them resentfully.

'Firn is right,' said Grodan. 'We can no longer follow our purpose. So how can this be the House of Truth?'

'It never was,' said Nian.

'What?' Rago jutted his ancient head forward like an angry goose. 'How dare you say such things? I have lived eighty years in this House, eighty years, and my mind has known things you barely dream of. I can control the skies, do you understand?'

'Yes,' said Nian. 'I understand. But you do not do it with Truth.'

'Ha!' said Rago. 'You don't know what you're talking about. You're a young ignoramus, that's all.'

'Who has found a way to reach other worlds,' said Bran, surprisingly.

Rago dismissed that with a swipe of a withered hand.

'The earthquake caused a rift that joined the worlds. It has happened before. The boy will have had no greater part in it than the Tarhun did. All he did was fall down a hole that was already dug.'

'And then return, to triumph over us,' pointed out Grodan.

'Yes,' said the deep voice of Bran. 'And now our

powers have shrunk and the worlds are huge and we are left naked upon them. What will happen if there is another earthquake? I am afraid.'

Nian's heart was beating fast.

'You must leave, then,' he said. 'As Varn and I are going to do.'

Varn, beside him, gasped, but there was a murmuring amongst the Lords, and Firn let out a cry of anguish.

'But what will happen to *us*? We are old! How should we live?'

Varn turned to Nian.

'Let's just go, now,' he said. 'Don't listen to them. We don't owe them anything. And they can't stop us.'

And that was true. Yes, Nian and Varn could walk out and leave these old men festering here uselessly, as between them they had for centuries. There was no reason for Nian to bother about them. Why should he care?

But even as he asked himself that question, he knew why. Because they had gifts, as he did. Because they had once been boys; because so much of their lives had been wrested from them and wasted already.

'You still have all your natural powers,' he told them. 'You have all those you had before the Tarhun took you. And the powers you have lost were useless, anyway.'

There was an indignant stirring at that.

'Insolent young puppy!' growled Rago, shooting out his scrawny tortoise neck. 'If I had my strength I'd—'

'But they *were* useless!' Nian exclaimed. 'A thousand years of searching, and nothing found. And as for the worlds . . . ' He actually laughed as he thought about his home among the valleys, and about Jacob's complicated town a whole world away—'you need not worry about the worlds, my Lords, for *the worlds are very well made.*'

'But how can a life dedicated to the Truth be useless?' demanded Rago, in a squall of fury. 'Once we understand the Truth of something we can control it. Use it.'

'No,' said Nian, urgently. 'Once you understand the Truth of something you can help it grow. You have not been seeking the Truth: you have been seeking to stunt things and bind them to your will.'

'That is ridiculous!' spluttered Rago. 'The boy is ignorant, foolish, a liar!'

But Tarq spoke, and now his voice was loud and clear.

'No, my Lord Rago,' he said. 'For consider: the foretellings have all been fulfilled. The House has been in decay for centuries; the statue in the garden has disappeared; and there is one amongst us who can fly. The boy is no liar: the boy is the Truth Sayer.'

There was silence in the House of Truth. And Nian felt another doom sweeping down upon him.

‖‖ ‖‖ ‖‖ ‖‖ ‖‖
‖‖ ‖‖ |

There was a deep silence in the Council Chamber. Then Bran spoke.

'To believe that the boy Nian is the Truth Sayer means discarding the work of many lives,' he said. 'And yet . . . and yet, I find I *do* believe it.'

But Nian was afraid: more afraid than he had been in all this endless day.

'It can't be me,' he said. 'I don't even *want* to save the House.' He turned to Varn pleadingly. 'Tell them it's not me!'

But Varn only sighed.

'I told you to come away at once,' he said wearily. 'I told you not to listen.'

'Varn!' said Nian, appalled, but Varn rounded on him in sudden anger.

'What would you have me say?' he demanded. 'You've just cast down a millennium of lies—do you want me to start a new one?'

'But I cannot be the Truth Sayer, because I am leaving,' said Nian, panic-stricken. 'I am leaving *now*. I'm going home—to my *home*. That's where I belong, don't you all understand? Where I can be truly myself. I *have to go!*'

He looked around at them all, but still he was afraid.

Then Tarq stepped forward, and though he was old and frail Nian realized that he did not know how to fight him.

'My son—'

'*No!*' said Nian, more fiercely still. '*Not your son!*' but he hated himself for saying it.

The old man flinched, but then he nodded, very sadly.

'That is true,' he said. 'I have no son, nor ever shall have. Yes, that is something I must remember. And have you other Truths for me, Nian?'

'Yes,' said Nian, with all the defiance he could muster. 'That you mustn't kidnap boys and imprison them here for ever. You must let them go home.'

Rago let out a great *harrumph* of contempt.

'But the Tarhun have endless trouble finding gifted boys as it is!' he sneered. 'The House would soon be empty if we let them go!'

Nian glared back at him.

'But if they learnt something useful, like healing, then their parents might be glad to send them here in the first place,' he snapped. 'And if they had holidays, you might find they returned of their own accord.'

There was a pause, and then Varn said, a little aggressively:

'But all that still means I can go home straight away, doesn't it?'

'Yes, of course,' said Nian. But then he remembered Varn up on the ledge with the tile in his hand, and he found himself adding: 'As soon as you have sworn not to use your gifts to harm others.'

Varn snorted, but then he thought for a moment, and nodded.

'All right. And when must I come back?'

'When you like.'

'But what if I *don't* like?'

'Then you stay at home,' said Nian.

There was silence amongst the Lords of the House of Truth, but Firn's brow was wrinkled.

'But what of the rest of us?' he asked, very worried. 'Some of us will have no homes, and are too old to work.'

Nian rolled his eyes in exasperation.

'There is always work to be done,' he said. 'The library is full of unread knowledge, and your powers need to be rebuilt from the foundations. And there is so much you have never seen. All of you, except the eldest and most infirm, should leave the House sometimes. Then perhaps you might even be able to use your gifts to help people.'

Grodan raised an eyebrow.

'Hm,' he said. 'It all sounds rather tiring.'

'I only said *sometimes*!' said Nian, irascibly. 'When you are tired, or if your powers fail you, you can come back to rest, can't you.'

There was a thoughtful pause.

'And what of the Tarhun?' asked Bran, at last. 'They will have no purpose.'

Nian thought about the Tarhun, and laughed.

'They are extremely greedy and devious,' he said. 'But I suppose that when there are lots of boys here, and many visitors, the Tarhun might be useful for looking after them.'

Tarq's skull-like face lit up in a smile.

'*Will* there be lots of boys?' he asked.

'Oh yes,' said Nian, who seemed suddenly able to see very clearly, and far into the distance. 'One day every village will have a man trained in this House to help them.'

The Lords looked at each other enquiringly, but Rago snarled and stuck out his lip.

'Lots of boys, and no mists of Wisdom to control them!' he exclaimed. 'We'll have hordes of noisy unruly children all over the place!'

'Yes,' said Nian. 'But you can give them places to be noisy. They can play in the garden. You can have part as a playground, and part to grow food, and part to be beautiful. Yes, and then you will all be able to walk in the garden every day.'

Rago was fairly spitting with outrage.

'What?' he demanded. 'Do you expect *me,* a Lord of the House of Truth who has dedicated himself to pure Wisdom for eighty years, to wander around gawping at *weeds*? What do you expect me to learn from that, may I ask?'

'Humility,' answered Nian, sweetly, and all the Lords laughed, except Rago, who looked profoundly astonished.

Bran stirred.

'This is the Truth,' he said. 'It fills me with hope. I shall go back to my father's house. It may be that he is still alive, and I should like to see him again. Then I shall travel in the world for a while, and then, perhaps, I shall return.'

'And I'm going to go home, too, just as fast as I can,' said Varn. 'I'm going to have servants waiting on me hand and foot, and I'm going to sit in the cutting room for hours, just smelling the silk and listening to the scissors.'

He grinned hugely, and Nian smiled back at him.

'I shall stay here,' said Tarq. 'I must get ready for all the boys who will be coming. I shall look forward to welcoming them.'

One by one the Lords chose what they would do: rebuild their powers; go out into the world; seek ancient wisdom in the library; tend the garden; heal; return to their homes.

'You give us hope, Truth Sayer,' said Firn, making an odd tortured face that might prove to be a smile, one day, with practice.

Nian nodded, and knew in his heart that he had done what he had had to do.

'But that is all I can give you,' he said. 'For I am going home.'

7

Jacob was wrapping up china figures and packing them into an ancient suitcase. The room was quiet apart from the rustle of newspaper, and suddenly it felt lonely. Terribly, terribly lonely.

No more sails cracking in a gale; no more baboons crashing through the forest canopy; no more yodelling of street vendors.

Jacob paused for a moment, just to feel sad.

And although the room was quiet, it wasn't silent: there were the sounds of the traffic outside, and Nan stomping about upstairs; there was something else, too.

Something rustling.

There was, there was! There was something behind the china cabinet.

And there, there—something was moving. It was no bigger than a mouse, but it *wasn't* a mouse.

It was coming out: an enormous electric-blue beetle.

An enormous electric-blue beetle *from another world*.

Jacob watched it, fascinated, as it ambled, tipping and swaying, through the tufts of the rug to the fire-place, and started eating the hearth kerb.

'Oi!' said Jacob, reaching out for it; then he noticed the extreme ease with which it was biting off chunks of wood, and thought again.

In the end he enticed the beetle into an old baked bean tin by baiting it with one of Robyn's pencils, and made a home for it on the front room mantelpiece in the old goldfish tank from the loft.

He called it Ringo.

The front room stayed peaceful, mostly, after that, but when Jacob put his ear right up against Ringo's tank he could hear things. All sorts of things: bells, or the cackling of hens, or rock concerts.

Sounds from other worlds, drawn in along the trail of something that had travelled further than Jacob could imagine.

He never told Dad, though.

‖‖ ‖‖ ‖‖ ‖‖ ‖‖
‖‖ ‖‖ ‖‖

Nian and Varn left the Council Chamber together.
Now they were to leave, the wide white corridors of
the House seemed suddenly to have bloomed into their
own spare beauty.

'We'll just get some provisions from the kitchen,'
said Varn, 'and then we'll be off.'

There was only bread to take. They each packed a
small oat sack with loaves, and then there was nothing to wait for. But they went first to find Tarq, to say
farewell.

'Go safely,' he said. 'I shall think of you both. You
will be welcome if you should return.'

'Oh, I suppose I might come back, sometime,' said
Varn, ungraciously. 'To visit. Just to see how things are
going. Perhaps I'll send you something from home:
food, and cloth for clothes.'

'Goodbye,' said Nian, steadily, and Tarq looked at
him and nodded, though with great sadness.

'Go, my friends,' he said, not saying *son*, as he had
been used to do. 'Be full of happiness.'

Their way lay together along the path that led down
the Holy Mountain. They hardly talked, for they were

used to being silent, and in any case they had little attention to spare from the mountain, and the sky, and the myriad things between. Nian had forgotten how many greens make up a countryside. He'd forgotten how the clusters of the wingtree seeds swayed ponderously in the wind, and how the wine bushes balanced sweet creamy saucers of blossom; he'd forgotten how fumbling the bees were, and how the stiff stems of the scratch-burrs nursed cups of water.

They came at last to the place where their paths parted, and they paused.

'It's only two days since we last said goodbye,' said Varn. 'And this time it's not for good, I hope. Would your family welcome a visit from a rich city gentleman, do you think? I'd like to see your home.'

'When I've told my family about all you've done for me they'll want you to stay for ever,' Nian replied. 'But I'll be the most glad of us all to see you.'

'Then I'll come, one day. Farewell, little Nian!'

Nian only laughed.

'Farewell, Varn. Go in happiness.'

Then they turned away from each other and walked resolutely towards their homes.

IIII IIII IIII IIII IIII
IIII IIII III

It was nearly two weeks before Nian came within
sight of his father's house, for he had to work for his
food for most of the way. He wove baskets in one
place, and scoured pans in another; in a third place
there was a little girl with a high fever. So he cured
her. The people there tried to give him gold, but he
would accept only food to get him home; even then
he saved some of the sweetmeats to share with Miri
and Tan.

He arrived at the farmyard gate one evening just as
the clouds were beginning to glow. He was tired, but
very happy, and for a while it was enough to lean on
the gate and feast his eyes on home.

As he stood watching, a girl stepped out of the
kitchen door carrying the log basket. She was tall and
well-built: one the men would notice. Nian found himself smiling, for this was his sister Miri, though she'd
grown up so much in the last year that he felt almost
shy of her.

The sight of the figure at the gate sent her hand
flying to her mouth in shock.

'*Nian!*' she gasped.

Nian kept smiling, though she'd turned as white as her head-cloth.

'I thought I'd come home,' he said, lamely enough.

Miri stood staring at him for so long that Nian almost became afraid he wasn't welcome, but then she gave a strange sort of shaken sigh and hurried over to the gate.

'Oh, Nian,' she said, but her voice was hushed and anxious. 'Oh, Nian, I never looked to see you again! I thought you were a ghost, especially . . . well, come in, come in.'

Nian unclasped the gate, but as he stepped through it he sensed something he'd never known there before. It stopped him in his tracks, and when he tried to take a step towards the house the strength of it pushed him back, brought him to a standstill. Impatient, he almost batted it aside, but instead he stopped and listened to it. And it was all grief, and frustration, and dreadful pity.

He looked sharply at Miri.

'What's happened?' he demanded.

Miri's eyes would not meet his.

'Oh, Nian,' she said, 'I'm sorry your homecoming should be like this. Everyone will be so happy you're here, we have spoken of you every day. But . . . but—'

'Is someone dead?' demanded Nian.

Tears brimmed from her eyes, but she hastily brushed them away with her sleeve: Nian's heart bumped with the familiarity of that childlike gesture.

'I mustn't cry,' she said. 'There's too much to do.'

Nian put a steadying hand on her arm.

'Tell me what's the matter,' he said. 'Someone is ill. Who is it?'

Miri gave up the effort of trying not to cry.

'It's Tan,' she blurted out. 'He caught his foot on a stone—it was just a graze, that was all—and now . . . '

'What? Gangrene?'

Miri shook her head and gave a long jerking sniff to try to stem her tears.

'They say his blood is poisoned,' she whispered.

Nian understood the feelings he'd sensed from the house, then. The green rocks of the mountains harboured many secrets, and a scratch could be enough to kill. Blood-poisoning took a swift hold, and led to convulsions, and terrified delirium, and death.

'Where is he, Miri?'

'In Father's room. Nian!'

Miri's eyes were so wide you could hardly see the grey round the black pupils. 'They talk of smothering him,' she said, in a small petrified whisper. 'They say it is kindest. But . . . oh, Nian, who could bear to do it?'

Nian gave her arm a reassuring squeeze and ran across the yard. He went through the kitchen, across the hall, and up the stairs. Once he reached the landing he could hear voices, and that gave him hope, for the sound of death is silence. Nian ran to the door of Father's room and pulled it open. Mother was kneeling on the floor and Tan was gasping noisily, breath after rasping breath, in her arms. And there, more tired and defeated than Nian

266

would have imagined possible, was Grandy, and Father was with her. He held a pillow in white-knuckled hands.

Nian went swiftly to stand in front of his brother. Tan's hair was dark with sweat, and his eyes were nearly closed, but he saw Nian.

Mother looked up, and gasped, and said something. Father and Grandy were saying things, too, asking questions, but Nian was focusing all his powers on Tan. He sensed Tan's fear first of all; then Nian delved deeper and discovered the minuscule creatures that had invaded Tan's body.

Nian, reminded of the mind-worms, flinched away, but then he forced himself to watch them properly. They were so many, so many. And what were they doing? Nian held his breath so that every part of himself could concentrate. The little creatures were in Tan's blood; they were spreading poison into each little cell.

Nian braced himself to fight them, but as he did he realized that Tan's body was fading, failing, fragile: a battle would burst it apart.

Fear swept over him. Was there nothing he could do, then, after all? He could make a path between the worlds, destroy a millennium of lies, so could he truly not help Tan? He had cured Jacob's grandmother—but she had been tough, not young and tender.

Tan had grown taller in the last year, and broader, though his body lay in his mother's indigo lap grey-tinged with weakness. Mother herself seemed diminished by her sorrow, almost ugly with it.

Beside herself with grief; near destroyed by it.

Yes. These little creatures that had invaded Tan really were like the black thought-worms the Lords had set on Nian. They were burrowing into Tan and isolating each little part of him by starving it of food and air. That was what was killing him.

These creatures were overpowering Tan, just as the lying power of the Lords had sought to overpower things. But still, lies need not be fought with lies. Nian had to nurture the Truth of Tan.

Nian knelt down beside his brother.

'I have come home,' he said, very clearly. 'And I am going to make you strong.'

Nian took Tan's hand from their mother's so that his powers could flow strongly into him.

'You are going to sleep,' he said. 'And you will sleep until you are strong again. Do you understand, Tan?'

Tan caught at the promise of rest so eagerly that his eyes had closed before Nian had finished speaking. Mother was asking more questions, but Nian was lowering Tan into a deeper and deeper slumber. Nian poured power into Tan until Tan was strong, stronger than the disease that was consuming him.

And then, at last, Nian sat back on his heels and turned to face his family.

It could not be a joyful reunion, not with Tan so ill. Mother seized him and hugged the breath out of him and asked shrill questions, but Nian gently disengaged himself.

'Someone must stay with Tan,' he explained. 'It may

be that the fever will increase, and if it does I must be called. Is there someone who will stay with him?'

'I will stay,' said Grandy. 'But, Nian, what have you done to him? Is there any chance for him, now?'

'I've made him strong, that's all. He'll still need nursing. But I think—I *think* he'll be all right.'

'And did you learn to do that on the mountain?' Mother asked. 'In the House of Truth?'

Nian thought of all he'd learned and done since the last time he'd been home, and he was amazed by how very much that was.

'I suppose I did, in a way,' he said.

'Then bless the House,' said Mother.

$$\text{卌 卌 卌 卌 卌}$$
$$\text{卌 卌 ||||}$$

Nian's return to his father's house was less happy than he'd hoped, but still it was full of pleasures. The food was so sumptuously and all-embracingly marvellous after a year in the House that sometimes Nian found his feet leaving the ground just at the scent of it.

Father showed him round the out-buildings and barns, and described in extreme detail everything that had happened during the last year. This was absorbingly interesting, but Nian wouldn't go any further from the house in case Tan needed his attendance.

Nian worked as much as he was able: he sharpened each scythe in preparation for the hay harvest and he checked over every strap of every harness.

And he thought.

He found he missed Varn considerably; in some ways he even missed Tarq. And sometimes, when he was off his guard, he found himself wondering if it was possible, as Robyn had said, to step from one world to another without shaking all the worlds apart. Nian drew diagrams in the dirt to try to understand it (for there was no hartskin in the place), but it remained tantalizingly beyond his understanding. He began to wonder if there was anything in the library of the House of Truth to help him . . . and then he grew frustrated because it was a week's journey away. He was even short with Miri when she brought him titbits to try to cheer him up. So he sat down to enjoy Grandy's stories, but they seemed florid and foolish, so he told his own story of his friends in another world.

Sheep? said everyone. *Did you hear them singing?*

But Miri was really most interested in the fashions, and Mother in the food. Father was intrigued by the idea of a world with too many people.

'They are wise, then,' he said, 'to preserve a little of everything. You can never tell what may be useful.'

That was unarguable, but its carefulness annoyed Nian. Almost everything annoyed Nian just then, so he plunged into a description of the other world's language to forget it.

'They were wicked people, then,' said Mother. 'You are well away from folk with such double tongues.'

'Not wicked,' said Nian, irritated again. 'They were kind lies, often, or sometimes necessary ones.'

'Well, I am just glad the worlds are peaceful again,' said Grandy. 'They've been keeping me awake with all their groaning and belly-aching.'

Nian smiled, but he found himself thinking a great deal about that strange fact that people who told lies were not always wicked.

A week and a day after Nian's arrival, Tan woke up properly. He was weak, but the fever was gone and he was quite himself again. He was soon able to sit up

271

and eat. And eat. And eat. Nian, inspecting him, judged that Tan was now five fingers taller than he was. Nian was surprised altogether at the change in Tan, for Tan seemed almost intelligent, at times: he certainly knew which crops grew best in which field, and which men were happiest at each task, and which of them worked well together.

The day Tan was well enough to walk around the farm Father ordered a feast to celebrate the return of both his sons. Nian, still suffering from a whole year of undernourishment, was not strong enough to work in the fields, so he helped in the kitchen instead, chopping vegetables and kneading dough, while the women bustled about in an anxious frenzy of baking and preparing. At one point, when his mother had presented him with a young mountain of knobbly sweetroots to scrub, he paused with his arms up to the elbows in muddy water and reminded himself that he was the Truth Sayer, and the most powerful person the world had ever known. Then his mother saw him slacking, so she snapped at him and told him to get on with his work.

About halfway down the mound of sweetroots he came to a decision.

Tan was dressing himself for the feast when Nian finally came up from the kitchen. Nian saw how strong Tan's shoulders were: compared with Tan's, his own were puny. He went to the press where the feast clothes were kept and got out the embroidered tunic and breeches that still fitted him.

'You can't know how good it is to be well again,' said Tan. 'How wonderful it is, just to breathe. And I owe it all to you. I won't forget it, Nian. Here. I've been saving this for you.'

It was a folded sash, piped in scarlet for the eldest son. Nian looked at it, and he remembered how proud he had been of it. He took it in his hands and ran his nail down all the carefully ironed-in folds, and he knew this sash meant that one day he'd be ruler of all this little world.

Nian smiled, and handed it back to his brother.

'You are our father's heir now,' he said. 'I must return to the House soon, so I won't be able to care for the farm as you will. Look after the land and people kindly, Tan.'

Tan stood, frozen between concern and amazement, with the sash hung loosely over his hands.

'But . . . will you really give up the farm and all your inheritance to me?' he asked. 'And go back to live with all those old Lords?'

'I have a lot to do there,' Nian answered, and as he spoke he was wondering what world was touching the garden now. What if every world was as different and wonderful as Jacob's? 'And anyway, you're stronger than me, and taller than me, and more suited to being a farmer in every way. But . . . I would be glad of one thing, Tan. A favour.'

'What is it?'

'I'd like to be able to come here, sometimes, when I'm tired. Will you allow me to stay here when I wish?'

'This is your home,' said Tan, simply, 'and I owe you my life. Whenever you come you will be welcome, and you shall have the seat of honour at the table, and we shall grieve when you leave us. Is that really all I can do?'

Nian thought. There was something else.

'There will be other Lords travelling through the valleys from now on,' he said. 'If one should come here, treat him kindly.'

'Can all the Lords cure sickness?'

'Well . . . they all have some powers of healing,' said Nian, a little doubtfully. 'And, yes, they'll be getting better at it once I start showing them what they're supposed to be doing. They're well-meaning enough, I suppose.'

'Then they'll be reverenced by everyone,' said Tan. 'And of course we'll treat them kindly: they'll be blessed throughout the land.'

And that was another prophecy about the Truth Sayer come true, Nian realized, in wonder. The Lords were to be blessed throughout the land: and it was his doing. What else might he do if he went back to the House and thought about things really properly?

'Here,' he said, 'let me help you.'

And he tied the sash in its careful folds around Tan's waist, and he felt as if he had been released from bonds.

274

8

The torch was nearly dead, but Jacob only needed it to work for a minute. He got the secateurs and went out into the garden to Dad's woodland patch and cut off six inches or so of ash tree. Ringo would eat more or less anything (especially loo roll), but Jacob felt he should have a constant supply of fresh wood to keep his mandibles active.

Jacob paused at the back door. Above him the sky was studded with the tiny points of a hundred stars, and there were hundreds, thousands, millions more, hidden by the distance, or the orange glow of the street lights.

Where was Nian, in all that lot?

Somewhere. Somewhere linked, if only in the most delicate and tenuous way, to the piece of ash Jacob held in his hand.

Jacob looked back on those extraordinary two days: the talcum-powder bomb, the statue in the front room, Douggie . . . and he found himself grinning. Nian would be all right. He was a fighter. Wherever he was, it'd take more than a handful of old monks to stop him.

Jacob nodded, suddenly quite certain. Nian would be fine in whatever *Wherever* he'd ended up.

Jacob raised a hand to the sky.

'Live well,' he murmured.

And went inside.

‖‖‖ ‖‖‖ ‖‖‖ ‖‖‖ ‖‖‖
‖‖‖ ‖‖‖ ‖‖‖

Nian stayed in his father's house one week more. He made it known that anyone who was ill could visit him for a cure, and in that way he got to see many of his old friends. The healthy ones he visited himself. He refused all offers of money, suggesting instead that a quantity of good food would be more than welcome at the House. In the end the villagers clubbed together and sent a whole wagonful creaking away up to the mountains.

Nian's farewells were sad, but not anything like as sad as the last time he'd left his father's house. For one thing he was sure he'd return, and for another he had a companion; this was a shy gangling boy of fourteen called Gow who'd been hiding his gifts in dread of the Tarhun. Now, however, he and his parents were keen for him to visit the House to learn all the lore of the Lords. Gow was wavering between fierce pride, fierce ardour, and fierce terror at the prospect of the House. Nian found this rather amusing.

They set off one fine morning when the suns were turning every drop of dew to a diamond sphere of brilliance. Nian stood at his father's gate and took a farewell look at the farmyard. This was a beautiful place, but then so was the garden of the House. And perhaps there would be many other beautiful places to see, in many other worlds.

He called to Gow, and turned to start the seven day journey to the House of the Lords of Truth.

And when he arrived, they made him very welcome.

Acknowledgements

I would like to thank Richard Cohen, Stephanie Coates, and Abbie Leeson, who know about police stations and being under arrest.

If I have got things wrong, however, it is not their fault.

Sally Prue first started making up stories as a teenager, when she realized that designing someone else's adventures was almost as satisfying as having her own. After leaving school Sally joined practically all the rest of her family working at the nearby paper mill. She now teaches piano and enjoys walking, painting, daydreaming, reading, and gardening. *Cold Tom*, Sally's first book, won the Branford Boase Award and the Smarties Prize Silver Award. Sally has two daughters and lives with her husband in Hertfordshire. *The Truth Sayer* is Sally's fifth novel for Oxford University Press.